Praise for

JILL SHALVIS

"She's a *New York Times* bestselling author, and there's a reason for her popularity: her writing is character-driven, accessible, and just the right kind of sultry."

—*Bustle*

"Engaging writing, characters that walk straight into your heart, touching, hilarious . . ."

—*Library Journal* on *One Snowy Night*

"Shalvis's sixth Heartbreaker Bay book spices up Christmas with a hint of humor, a dash of suspense, and a whole lot of naughty fun under the mistletoe. The characters come alive in this lighthearted, fun story written for cold winter nights."

—*Publishers Weekly* on *Hot Winter Nights*

"With her Heartbreaker Bay books, Shalvis has created a terrific crew of friends, each more lovable (and deserving of love) than the last."

—*Entertainment Weekly* on *Chasing Christmas Eve*

Also by Jill Shalvis

Wildstone Novels
LOVE FOR BEGINNERS • THE FOREVER GIRL
MISTLETOE IN PARADISE (novella)
THE SUMMER DEAL • ALMOST JUST FRIENDS
THE LEMON SISTERS • RAINY DAY FRIENDS
THE GOOD LUCK SISTER (novella)
LOST AND FOUND SISTERS

Heartbreaker Bay Novels
WRAPPED UP IN YOU • PLAYING FOR KEEPS
HOT WINTER NIGHTS • ABOUT THAT KISS
CHASING CHRISTMAS EVE
ACCIDENTALLY ON PURPOSE
THE TROUBLE WITH MISTLETOE • SWEET LITTLE LIES

Lucky Harbor Novels
ONE IN A MILLION • HE'S SO FINE • IT'S IN HIS KISS
ONCE IN A LIFETIME • ALWAYS ON MY MIND
IT HAD TO BE YOU • FOREVER AND A DAY
AT LAST • LUCKY IN LOVE • HEAD OVER HEELS
THE SWEETEST THING • SIMPLY IRRESISTIBLE

Animal Magnetism Novels
STILL THE ONE • ALL I WANT • THEN CAME YOU
RUMOR HAS IT • RESCUE MY HEART
ANIMAL ATTRACTION • ANIMAL MAGNETISM

HOLIDAY EVER AFTER

ONE SNOWY NIGHT, HOLIDAY WISHES &
MISTLETOE IN PARADISE

JILL SHALVIS

AVONBOOKS

An Imprint of HarperCollins*Publishers*

"One Snowy Night." Copyright © 2016 by Jill Shalvis.
"Holiday Wishes." Copyright © 2017 by Jill Shalvis.
"Mistletoe in Paradise." Copyright © 2020 by Jill Shalvis.

HOLIDAY EVER AFTER. Copyright © 2021 by Jill Shalvis. All rights reserved. Printed in the United States of America. No part of this book may be used or reproduced in any manner whatsoever without written permission except in the case of brief quotations embodied in critical articles and reviews. For information, address HarperCollins Publishers, 195 Broadway, New York, NY 10007.

First Avon Books mass market printing: November 2021

Print Edition ISBN: 978-0-06-311500-2
Digital Edition ISBN: 978-0-06-311501-9

Cover design by Nadine Badalaty
Cover art by Shane Rebenschied
Cover images © iStock/Getty Images; © Shuttterstock; © Adobe Stock

Avon, Avon & logo, and Avon Books & logo are registered trademarks of HarperCollins Publishers in the United States of America and other countries.

HarperCollins is a registered trademark of HarperCollins Publishers in the United States of America and other countries.

21 22 23 24 25   LSC   10 9 8 7 6 5 4 3 2 1

Contents

HOLIDAY EVER AFTER

ONE SNOWY NIGHT

Chapter One

CHRISTMAS EVE had the nerve to show up just like it did every year: way too quickly and with ridiculous fanfare.

The nerve.

Rory Andrews stood in the courtyard of the Pacific Pier Building in San Francisco, surrounded by sparkly holiday lights and enough garlands to give the place its own ozone, and told herself things could be worse.

She just wasn't sure how.

It was the unknown, she decided. Because this year, unlike the past six, she'd be spending Christmas with her family, a thought that caused a swarm of butterflies to take flight in her belly.

Not an uncommon feeling since she'd turned twenty-three a few months back and decided it was time to become a person she could be proud of if it killed her. And given the guy leaning against one of the lamp poles clearly waiting for her, arms crossed, frown in place, it just might.

Max Stranton. At his side sat Carl, his huge, eternally hungry, adorable Doberman.

"No," she said, not to Carl but to Carl's owner. Who was not lovable. "No way."

As always when their gazes locked, Max's was a disconcerting mix of heat and . . . something else that she couldn't quite figure out, as he was good at hiding when he wanted to be. She never quite knew how to take the heat because it seemed reluctant. He was attracted to her but didn't want to be.

Ditto. He made her knees wobble. And also a couple of other inner reactions that shouldn't be happening in public.

"Merry Christmas to you too, Rory," he said, and damn. It wasn't just his eyes. His voice was rough and sexy, and for that matter, so was the rest of him.

He worked for an investigations and security firm in the building. Basically he and the rest of his team were fixers and finders for hire. To say that Max was good at his job was an understatement. He stood there looking like sex-on-a-stick with a duffel bag slung over a broad shoulder, his dark hair two weeks past needing a cut, and the icy wind of an incoming storm plastering his clothes to a body that could be registered as a lethal weapon.

"What are you doing here?" she asked calmly even if her heart was anything but, pounding all the way up to her throat and ears because she knew. She knew *exactly* why he was here. "I don't need a ride home."

A flash of wry humor slid in with all that siz-zling heat. "Because you'd rather take two buses and a train than get into my truck with me?" he asked.

Well yes, actually.

Living and working in San Francisco was a dream come true for her. She'd turned her life around in the past few years but she still had some deep regrets, one of them being how she'd run away at age seventeen. This was something her wonderful but nosy boss Willa had talked her into facing once and for all, so she'd called home. She'd promised her stepdad she'd come for Christmas to surprise her mom and three half sisters. He'd ex-pressed surprise and then doubt, both with good reason.

Rory had made promises to come home before, and . . . hadn't. Every time she'd flaked. It'd been fear and anxiety, but she was ready to face all that now and she'd told him so. She'd even offered to pick up the gift he'd ordered for her mom from the city and get it home before dawn on Christmas morning.

If she managed to do so, all would be forgiven.

Not that he'd said so in those words, but she felt the pressure all the same. She wanted to do this; she was ready to do this.

"It's Christmas Eve," Max said now, keys in hand. "I just finished a job. I'm leaving to spend a few days with my family. I'm going right past your mom's house."

Which was in Tahoe, where Max had also been raised—four hours north in good weather, which wasn't going to be tonight. Her stomach jangled. Fate or Karma or whatever was in charge of such things was a cruel master, having her first crush of all people, the *one* guy on the entire planet who made her feel like that young, neglected, bullied, unwanted teen all over again, be the only smart ride home tonight.

Max's body language said he was relaxed and laid-back as he watched her think too much, but she knew better. He spent most of his days rooting out the asshats of San Francisco. He was a chameleon when he wanted to be, a sharp one. Nothing got by him.

Well, except one thing, of course—he had no idea that once upon a time for her the sun had risen and set on his smile. She'd flown under the radar in high school. Hell, she'd flown under the radar in life, and she'd been really good at it. Plus Max had never had a shortage of girls who were interested in him so he'd had no reason to look past any of the ones throwing themselves at his feet in order to see her.

But that was then. In the here and now, things felt . . . different. Whether either of them wanted to admit it or not, they'd taken notice of each other, and even more unbelievably, she often caught him watching her with what felt like heat and desire.

Not that he'd ever made a move.

"Are you ready?" he asked.

The ten-million-dollar question. "As I'll ever be," she said.

"I don't get it." His tone was age-old male bafflement with a dash of annoyance. His eyes were a very dark shade of green. They looked almost black now in the night. "I had to find out from Willa that you needed a ride. You could've asked me yourself. You should have asked me, Rory."

Right. Because they talked so much. But before she could say that, or even pet Carl, her favorite dog on the planet, a woman ran out of the convenience store on the corner, breathless and adorable in a red apron and Santa hat.

"Just wanted to tell you something," she said to Max and flung herself into his arms.

He had little choice but to catch her, and she laughed and kissed him, taking her time about it too.

While they were lip-locked, Carl gave one deep bark and the woman finally pulled back, grinning wide as she said to both man and his dog, "Merry Christmas! See you next year!"

And then she vanished back into the store where she worked, which Rory knew because she often bought ice cream there after a long day at work.

Max shook his head but was looking amused. Rory searched his gaze, looking to see if Santa's Helper caused that same breathless heat she'd gotten used to seeing when he looked at *her*.

It wasn't there.

She took a deep breath at that, not wanting to

acknowledge it as relief. She shouldn't care that he hadn't felt an overwhelming hunger for that girl.

"Let's do this," he said.

"This" of course being the unwelcome chore of giving her a ride. "Look, I'm not sure this is a good idea." Because honestly? Two buses and a train would be a piece of cake in comparison, never mind that she didn't have the money for that.

"Rory," he said, a hint of impatience in his tone.

Once again she looked into his eyes, and at what she saw, her heart stopped on a dime.

The heat was back. For her.

"This isn't exactly my idea of fun either," he said. "Trust me."

Ha. She wasn't exactly on the trust program with any man but especially not this one. Not that she was about to tell *him* that.

Max's attention was suddenly drawn to the alley and the man standing in it. Old Man Eddie was a fixture of the Pacific Pier Building every bit as much as the fountain in the center of the courtyard. Everyone who worked here did their best to take care of him, including Rory.

"Hold on a sec," Max said and moved toward Eddie, who was wearing a sweatshirt with a peace sign and Hawaiian-print board shorts, his medical marijuana card laminated and hanging from a lanyard around his neck.

"Merry Christmas, man," Rory heard Max say and then he slipped the old man something that she suspected was cash.

And damn if her heart didn't execute a slow roll in her chest, softening for him, which didn't exactly make her night.

Old Man Eddie pocketed the money and grinned at Max, and then they did one of those male hugs that involved back slapping and some complicated handshake.

Ignoring them, Rory reached into her bag and pulled out some red ribbon. A big part of her job at South Bark Mutt Shop was grooming. Carl had been her first client earlier that morning and afterward, she'd woven a piece of the festive ribbon around his collar, which he'd seemed to love, but there was no ribbon in sight now. Crouching in front of him, she replaced it, looping it in a jaunty bow at the side of his neck. "There," she said. "Better, right? The girls'll be falling all over themselves to get you."

Carl gave her a big, slurpy lick along her chin. Then he nosed her bag, sniffing out the fact that she had goodies in there. "Later," she promised.

"No," Max said, coming back to them. "Hell no. Take that thing off, you're going to kill his image."

Rory rose to her full height, which still wasn't even close to Max's. She barely made it up to his shoulder and, dammit, she wished she was in heels. "A ribbon doesn't emasculate him, and even if it did, there's nothing wrong with that."

"Of course there's not," he said. "But female or male, he's a working dog and in our business he—or *she*—has to be tough and badass. A bow doesn't exactly say 'stop and drop or I'll *make* you stop and drop.' "

Okay, so maybe he had a point there. "It's Christmas Eve," she said. "I think he can take the night off of being tough and badass, can't he?"

Max blew out a sigh that spoke volumes on what he thought of the matter—and her—and headed for the wrought iron gate to the street, stopping to hold it open for her.

As she passed through, their bodies brushed together, his hard as stone and yet somehow also deliciously warm, and hers . . . softened. There was no other word for it.

At the contact, he sucked in a breath and jerked her gaze to his. And then she was sucking in a breath too, frozen in place, held there by the shocking chemistry that always seemed to sizzle between them, just under the surface.

She had no idea what to do with that, but damn . . .

Max muttered something to himself about bad timing and idiocy before leading her to his truck, parked at the curb.

Which brought up the question—just how badly did she want to get home? Bad, she could admit. She needed to make amends. She needed forgiveness for being such a horrible, unhappy, terrible teenager, even if it meant swallowing her pride and taking the ride from Max.

She got into the truck in tune to a growing wind and a clap of thunder in the far distance. Max settled Carl in the backseat and then leaned in to buckle him in, giving the big dog an 'ol kiss on the snout as he did. The unexpected action was such a sweet, gentle thing to do, and such a dichotomy from his usual stoic badassery that Rory found herself smiling.

Max caught her expression as he slid in behind the wheel. "What?" he asked.

"What what?" she asked.

"You're smiling."

"Is there a law against that?"

He put his truck in gear and pulled out into the street. "No, but you don't usually aim it at me."

"You've got that backward, don't you?" she asked, deciding not to mention that she'd been aiming the smile at Carl.

Max slid her a look that sizzled her nerve endings and then redirected his attention to the streets. San Francisco was looking pretty gorgeous in her Christmaswear, a myriad of lights decorating the buildings, light poles wrapped in garlands. As they made their way through the busy district and got on the freeway, it began to rain. Hard.

The sound of the rain pinging off the truck was loud, echoing in the interior. Max didn't speak and she blew out a breath. It was going to be a long ride home. *Home.* Just the word brought more than a few nerves. And nerves made her babble. "So what's your problem with me?"

Nothing from Max but a slight tightening of his scruffy jaw.

"Can't decide on one thing?" she asked.

"I don't have a problem."

Okaaaay. She searched for something else to say, anything at all to draw him out because the silence was going to drive her batty. "Heard you guys had to jump off the roof of a building to catch some bad guys for the good guys yesterday."

He smiled at the memory as if it'd been fun. "Can't talk about work," he said.

Right. "So who's the chick who tried to swallow your tongue?"

He choked out a laugh but didn't speak, which just plain old pissed her off. She knew damn well he could talk; she'd seen him do it plenty. But he absolutely wasn't interested in conversation with her. Fine. Point served, silence it was. She went with it for all of three minutes, but in the end she couldn't do it. Turning in her seat, she studied her driver.

Tall, hard, and lean, he'd definitely changed since they'd gone to high school together. She'd left home immediately after her junior year. She'd eventually gotten a job and taken her GED but she hadn't kept up with anyone from Tahoe. Mostly because she'd had such a crap time growing up. She'd needed to get away with a clean slate, badly, and frankly there'd been no one she'd wanted to stay in touch with.

Except maybe . . . secretly . . . Max himself, a fact she'd take to her grave, thank you very much. They'd had a science class together, that was it;

nothing memorable for him, she was certain. But he'd been kind to her, twice taking her on as a lab partner when no one else had wanted the shy, bad-at-science wallflower, and she'd never been able to forget it. Or him. "So what college did you end up at?" she asked.

Surprisingly enough, *this* got her a reaction. He looked at her across the dark console, rain and wind and city lights slashing as harshly across his features as his voice sounded when he asked, *"Are you kidding me?"*

Chapter Two

MAX HADN'T meant to respond to Rory's questions at all but that last one—*where had he gone to college?*—cut through all his good intentions and lit the fuse of his rare temper.

She couldn't be serious. She knew damn well what she'd done to him, what she'd cost him.

She had to.

Didn't she?

He glanced at her, and the intensity that was always between them ratcheted up a notch, something he'd have sworn wasn't possible.

"Why would I be kidding you?" she asked.

Like he was going to go there with her, but at whatever was in his expression along with the tone of his voice, Carl whined.

Rory narrowed her eyes at Max, clearly blaming him for upsetting the dog, before she twisted, going up on her knees to reach over the back of her seat for Carl.

His dog, hampered by his seatbelt, whined again and leaned into her touch.

Rory made a soft sound in her throat and clicked

out of her seatbelt to wrap her arms around the big oaf—a fact Max knew only because he could see her both in his rearview mirror and over his shoulder. He watched as she loved up on his big, slobbery dog, not seeming to care one little bit when Carl smiled and drooled all over her pretty sweater.

Most women didn't like Carl.

Which didn't matter in the least to Max. Women came and went, if he was very lucky. And yeah, he'd been luckier than most in that regard. But there'd been no keepers, much to his family's ever loving dismay. So far, Carl was his only keeper.

And Carl clearly loved and adored Rory.

That wasn't the problem. Nope, the problem was that Rory seemed completely clueless to what she'd done to Max. She'd ruined his life and she'd either forgotten or she didn't care. The crazy thing was that he'd hardly known her. The only reason he'd even known her name was because he'd been her lab partner a few times. But though he'd enjoyed her company, she'd ignored him outside of class.

And back then she hadn't been his type anyway. He'd been an unapologetic jock, and he'd be the first to admit that he'd been enough of an ass to enjoy the perks of that—including going out with girls known to enjoy sleeping with the most popular athletes.

He glanced in the rearview mirror again. Huge mistake. All he could see was Rory's heart-stopping ass covered in snug, faded denim that outlined her every curve, and his mouth actually watered, wanting to bite it.

In the time that they'd both been working in the city, he'd come to realize that not only had she outgrown her shyness, but she was smart, resourceful, and funny. If he didn't resent their past so much, he'd probably have asked her out a long time ago.

But he did resent their past, which left him both driven nuts by her presence and also somehow . . . hungry for her. Which meant it was official: he'd lost his mind.

If he'd ever had it in the first place.

He glanced at the very nice view again and the wheels of his truck hit the edge of his lane, giving off a loud whump whump whump. "Shit," he muttered and jerked the truck back into the lane.

Smooth, real smooth, he thought with self-disgust.

At the motion of his truck swerving, Rory nearly slid into his lap.

"Sorry," she gasped, bracing one hand on his shoulder, the other high up on his thigh, using them to shove clear of him.

He could still feel the heat of her hands on him as she flopped back in her seat, hair in her face. She shoved it clear and then bent over and started rifling through the huge purse at her feet.

The movement slid her sweater north and her jeans south, revealing a two-inch strip of the creamy white skin of her lower back.

And two matching dimples that made his mouth water again.

"What the hell are you doing?" he managed to ask.

"Nothing." She straightened, coming up with a dog biscuit, which she tossed back to Carl. The dog snapped it out of thin air, practically swallowing it whole, and then licked his chops.

"You carry bones with you?" he asked in surprise.

"Of course," she said, like *didn't everyone?*

His phone buzzed an incoming call. He answered it via speaker but before he could say a word, his elder, know-it-all sister Cass spoke.

"I know you're on your way," she said, her voice blaring out from his truck's speakers. "So I'll be quick. Two things. One, the weather is atrocious and the roads up here are an epic disaster already so please be careful, and two, don't forget that we've got a promise between us."

"Cass—"

"No excuses," she said. "The next girl you feel something for, anything at all, you have to go for it, no exceptions. That's my Christmas present and I just wanted to remind you of that. And since I'm assuming you're going to say you've felt nothing, you should know I've got you covered."

Max didn't bother to groan. Nor did he look at Rory, who he could sense straightening in her seat with interest. "What have you done, Cass?"

"Me?" she asked innocently. "Nothing."

Yeah, and he was Santa Claus. *"Cass."*

Her sigh echoed in the truck interior. "Okay, fine, I might have invited a friend—"

"No," he said.

"Come on. Kendall's cute, smart, gainfully employed, and she has a crush on your dog."

"How the hell does she know Carl?"

"Honestly, Max? Are you seriously not reading my Facebook messages?"

No. He wasn't.

"I started a Facebook page for Carl weeks ago," Cass said. "He's already got a thousand likes."

If he hadn't been driving into a downpour with hurricane-force winds, he might've taken his hands off the wheel to rub his temples where a headache was forming. "I'm disconnecting you now," he warned, ignoring Rory's snort.

"So that's a yes on Kendall, right?"

"It's a firm *hell no*," he said.

Cass was silent a beat, thinking. Never a good thing for Max. "So . . . there *is* someone you're feeling something for," she said.

He nearly laughed. Yes. Yes, he was feeling something for the woman sitting next to him but it sure as hell wasn't what Cass was hoping for.

"Even a little spark of attraction counts," Cass warned. "You promised, Max. And you never break promises."

True story. He never broke promises.

"Max? Is there someone, then?"

Max slid a gaze across the console and found

Rory staring at him, her dark brown eyes swirling with emotions that he couldn't possible put a finger on without a full set of directions. She was beautiful in the girl-next-door way, meaning she had absolutely zero idea of her own power. In fact, Rory had always seemed completely oblivious of her looks. In high school, she'd been thin but had worn clothes that had tended toward shapeless, which had allowed her to be invisible as she'd clearly liked to be. She was still thin but had acquired curves in all the right places now, shown off by clothes that actually fit her. Her long hair was wavy and had its own mind. She hadn't tried to tame it, letting it flow in dark brown waves to her breasts. If she was wearing makeup, he couldn't see any.

What he had no problem seeing was her interest in his response to his sister.

Okay, yes, so he felt a physical attraction to her. And he'd felt that response more than once. A lot more, if he was being honest with himself, but he'd hidden it. Or so he hoped, telling himself it was nothing more than a natural male response to a female form. That was it. Because he wasn't attracted to Rory—unless you count the attraction of strangling her.

He shifted, knowing he was lying to himself.

"Max?" Cass asked.

"Bad reception," he said and disconnected the call, understanding damn well he'd pay for that later.

Rory snorted, amused.

He ignored that and her, and concentrated on the roads. Which were indeed shit.

"You could've told her about Santa's Helper, your girlfriend from the convenience store," Rory said casually.

He slid her a quick look. "Tabby's not my girlfriend," he said.

"So you kiss all the store clerks then?"

He rolled his eyes. He and Tabby weren't complicated. They were friends, with the very occasional added "benefits," but neither of them were interested in more. "Tabby's not in the picture."

"Does *she* know that?"

"Here's an idea," he said. "How about you make it my Christmas present to stop with the twenty questions?"

She turned to the window, shoulders squared.

Ah, hell. Now he felt like an asshole, but he had to admit, he did appreciate the silence.

About an hour up the highway, the rain turned to slush. He knew it wouldn't be much longer before they hit snow, which didn't bother him any. He'd grown up driving off-road vehicles and boats, and his dad often proudly said Max could drive a semi into an asscrack. And it was true, he could drive anything anywhere under any conditions. Where the danger and unknown came in was from the other idiots on the road.

Luckily tonight there was a shortage of them. They had the roads to themselves, probably because only the hearty would even dare try to be out in this insanity.

At the halfway mark, he stopped for fuel. Before he pumped gas, he tried to take Carl out, wanting him to do his business now so they wouldn't have to make another stop. "Let's go."

Carl curled up tight on his seat, eyes closed, playing possum. Carl didn't like snow very much. Max looked at Rory.

Rory shrugged.

"Come on," he said to Carl. "This'll be your last chance for a few hours."

Nothing from Carl.

"Now," Max said.

Carl, still not opening his eyes, only growled low in his throat.

From the passenger seat, Rory chuckled. "Is it like looking in a mirror?" she asked.

"Funny." Except not. He lowered his face to the dog's. "If you get up right this minute, I've got a doggie cookie—"

Before he'd even finished the sentence, Carl jumped up and out of the truck without a backward glance. "How about you?" he asked Rory. "You need a pit stop?"

She looked out the window into the snowy mess. "I'm good."

"Not even for a doggie cookie?"

She smiled but shook her head.

Whatever. Not his problem.

She did, however, try to give him cash for gas

when he came back with Carl, which Max flatly re-fused. He knew she was strapped, that she barely made ends meet. He also knew he was lucky as hell to have a great job with great pay, and yeah, that great pay was because his job could be dan-gerous, but he was good at what he did. And even if he hadn't landed a great job that he loved, he had his family. The entire nosy bunch would do any-thing for him and he knew it.

Rory didn't have that kind of support. She'd had it rough growing up. Her dad had never been around and her mom had remarried when Rory had been young. Her stepdad was a good guy, but 100 percent no-nonsense. He could be a real hard-ass, a stickler for obedience and all that. Rory had three half sisters, all sweet kids but quiet and meek.

Rory was the opposite of quiet and meek, and she hadn't fit in. As far as he knew, she'd left school after their junior year and had never been back. And after what she'd done to him, he'd told him-self he'd been more than fine with that.

But it didn't mean that he hadn't worried more than a little bit. Or that he wasn't aware of how hard it was for her to make it on her own, in San Francisco no less, a very expensive city. She worked at South Bark Mutt Shop and she also went to night school, and he knew she lived with a couple of roommates and still barely made ends meet. He didn't like to think about how she must struggle just to keep food in her belly. So no, he wasn't about to take her damn gas money.

He'd just started pumping the gas when his phone buzzed an incoming call. Willa ran South Bark and was Rory's boss. She was also the one who'd asked him to give Rory a ride to Tahoe, clearly having no idea that Max and Rory had gone to school together and had history. A bad history.

"How's the ride going?" Willa asked.

Max leaned against his truck. "Well, we haven't killed each other yet."

Willa didn't laugh.

"You know I'm kidding, right?" *Sort of . . .*

"Max." Willa's voice was quiet. Serious. "There are things I probably should've told you about Rory."

"You mean about the chip on her shoulder?" he asked wryly. "Yeah, I'm aware."

"She's earned that chip, Max. The hard way."

"And let me guess. You're going to fill me in."

"She's smart, so smart, Max. She'll fool you if you let her."

He shook his head and hunkered beneath the overhang, trying to avoid getting snow in his face while he waited for his gas tank to fill. "What does that even mean?"

"She's been with me for six years—"

"Working in your shop, I know," he said, impatient to get out of the snow, back in the truck and on the road.

"But what you don't know is how she came to me."

Actually, he did. Rory had pretty much ran away from home and—

"It was late one night," Willa said. "I was on a walk through the Marina Green when I found a girl in the park, sick as a dog from a drug someone had dumped in her drink."

Max froze. This was something he didn't know, although he wished he had because he'd have gladly hunted down the asshole who'd drugged her and he'd have—

"I'm not telling you this to make you mad," Willa said quietly. "I just want you to understand the chip."

He let out a long, purposeful breath. "What happened?"

"I took her to the hospital, helped her recover from events that she can't remember to this day, and gave her a job. But it wasn't easy. It took her a long time to learn to trust me."

Imagining what she must've suffered and reeling from that, Max couldn't even speak.

"Basically, I bullied her back to life," Willa said. "And lately she's been really . . . okay. Even happy."

Max knew this to be true. He'd seen Rory in the courtyard of their building, smiling and laughing with friends. He'd seen her with the animals in Willa's shop, specifically with Carl, who loved and adored her. And the reason he kept seeing her was because in spite of himself, he'd been drawn to her and he'd made sure their paths crossed. Often.

Shit.

He peered inside his truck, expecting to see Rory hunched over her phone, but there was no phone in sight. Instead she had her head bent to his dog, who was in her lap. All 100 plus pounds of him, big head on her shoulder.

He went back to the overhang. "Why are you telling me all this?" he asked Willa.

"Because I know there's something between you. A chemistry. We've all seen it, Max, the way you come by the shop with Carl for more groomings than you need, making sure to do it when Rory is there."

"Maybe I just love my stupid dog," he said, not happy to hear that he'd been that transparent when it came to his uncomfortable and complicated feelings for Rory.

"Oh, I know that's also true," Willa said smugly. "But that's not why you tip her so much. Look, I can tell by your tone I'm annoying you, so let me make it count. I know that you're trustworthy or you wouldn't be working for Archer. I guess I'm just hoping you can also be . . . gentle."

Max pressed his thumbs into his eye sockets. "Willa—"

"I know. You're big and badass and tough, and I get it, you don't do gentle. But maybe, for Rory, you could try."

Once again he looked in the truck. Rory was talking to Carl, smiling while she was at it. But once upon a time, not so long ago, she'd been hurt. Badly. And that killed him. *Fuck*. "Yeah. I guess I could try."

He heard Willa suck in a breath clogged with

emotion. "Merry Christmas, Max," she said softly. "You deserve it."

Actually, there was someone who deserved it far more and the hell of it was, it was the last person he'd expected it to be, and she was sitting in his truck hugging his big, silly dog.

Chapter Three

W<small>HEN</small> M<small>AX</small> opened the truck door a few minutes later and found Carl in his seat, he gave the dog a long look.

Carl hefted out a huge sigh and got into the back.

"Thank you, Carl," Rory said pointedly with a glance at Max that said he was clearly an idiot.

Max was an indeed an idiot, but not for not thanking his dog.

He was going to do as Willa had asked. He was going to be . . . *Christ* . . . gentle, even if it killed him. And it might. He was also going to get his own emotions under control, because at the moment he was filled with a cold fury over what Rory had suffered and he had nowhere to vent it.

"You were on the phone," Rory said.

"I was."

She looked at him, clearly waiting for more, her pretty eyes not giving much away. She was so petite a good wind could blow her away, but that analogy implied she was fragile.

Rory was anything but fragile, and in fact her

inner strength was even more attractive to him than her beauty.

"It was Willa," he said, willing to give her that. Besides she was more curious than a cat and he wanted to appease that curiosity and fast, before she figured out the rest.

She looked at him, surprised. "What did she want?"

Shit. On top of curious as a cat, she was like Carl with a damn bone. He twisted around to buckle Carl back in and then put on his own seatbelt. He turned the engine over and cranked up the radio.

Rory turned it off. "She already made you drive me, so what now?"

"Nothing."

Rory turned in her seat to fully face him. "Was she checking to see if we'd killed each other?"

He smiled at that, a thought that had been so close to his own, but she narrowed her eyes, not amused. "What did she want, Max?"

He went to put the truck in gear but she leaned into him to turn off the engine and grab his keys. Her breast brushed against his arm, giving him another zap of awareness.

"Come on," she said. "This is Willa we're talking about. I love her, but she's incapable of not sticking her nose in where it doesn't belong, especially when it comes to me. What did she want?"

Shit, it'd been two minutes and he was already regretting his "gentle" promise. He looked her right in the eyes. "Nothing."

Her eyes went to little slits. "Liar." She opened her door, revealing that the slush had turned to snow, as she swung his keys from her fingers. "Tell me or say goodbye to your keys."

"That'll strand you too," he pointed out.

She raised her eyebrows and he got the message. She didn't care.

"Fine," he said. "She told me to be nice to you. Actually, she said gentle." While she gaped at that, he snagged the keys from her lax fingers, feeling like an asshole when he leaned into her, reaching past her to slam her door shut.

She didn't shrink back, which meant that their bodies once again bumped up against each other, and it was like they knew what his brain couldn't seem to comprehend—he wanted her. He was a little thrown by that, and the now familiar zing of electricity, only slightly mollified to realize by the way her breath hitched that she felt it too.

"If you even try to be *gentle*," she said, "I'll get out and walk."

He pinched the bridge of his nose and laughed. He couldn't help it. She drove him insane. "Got it."

"I mean it."

"I believe you."

"Good," she said, sounding only slightly appeased. "Now tell me what she told you to make you agree to such a thing."

Christ, she was good. "How do you know she told me anything?"

"Again, it's Willa," she said. She crossed her

arms and stared at him, and for a second he was pretty sure she could see right inside his head and read his mind. "She told you something to make you feel sorry for me," she guessed.

He schooled his features into a blank face, or so he hoped. "I don't feel sorry for you," he said.

"Ha!" she cried, pointing at him. "She did! What was it? That I applied for an internship at a local vet, which I need for the animal tech credential I want, and got turned down flat for lack of credible references?"

Shit. No, he hadn't known that and his heart twisted for her. "Why didn't you ask someone to give you a reference?" he asked. "Archer, Joe, Spence, Finn . . . me? Any one of us would've jumped to help you."

She hadn't taken her eyes off of him. "Okay," she said slowly. "So it wasn't that."

Yeah, this conversation was about to go south fast. He reached to start the engine again because no way did he want this little guessing game to take a dark turn, which it would if she landed on the truth.

"There was only one other thing she could've told you that would have made you feel sorry enough for me to give me a ride," she said, staring at him. "But if she'd told you that, I think I'd be able to tell."

He met her gaze and she gasped softly, her eyes holding his prisoner. "Oh my God," she whispered, leaning back away from him. "Damn her."

"You were attacked in the park when you first landed in San Francisco," he said quietly, finding it a shocking effort to keep his voice calm. "That shouldn't have happened to you. It shouldn't happen to *anyone*."

She turned away. "We're not discussing this."

"Did you press charges?"

She looked out into the starry night. "Drive."

"Rory, please tell me he's rotting in a jail cell."

"Drive, dammit."

"Hang on a sec—"

"I didn't press charges and he's not rotting in a jail cell because I don't remember what he looks like!" she burst out. "I accepted a drink from a stranger, he drugged me, and I remember nothing. Not his face, not anything about him, and not a single second of that night at all. So no, I didn't turn him in. I had nothing to turn in. I was an idiot, okay? I was a complete idiot and I paid the price, and now if you don't mind, I don't want to talk about it ever again."

"I get that, but—"

"Not. Ever. Again," she said tightly. "And I mean it, Max. Bring it up and I'm out. I'll walk to Tahoe, I don't care." She turned to him then, eyes blazing with strength and temper. "We clear?"

Her strength was . . . amazing. "Crystal," he said quietly.

She nodded and relaxed marginally. "Good. And one more thing. If you so much as try to be gentle or handle me with kid gloves, I'll kick your

ass. And I could do it too—your boss taught me
some mean moves."

He believed her. If Archer had taught her then
she was lethal, and he was glad for it. No one
would take advantage of her again. He started the
truck and navigated their way through the falling
snow back onto the highway, where they left most
of civilization behind as they hit the wild Sierras.

It was always a surreal thing to drive in heavy
snow in the dark of night. In the black landscape,
the snow came at them in diagonal slashing lines
across the windshield. The road narrowed to two
lanes, winding back and forth in tight S-turns as
they began to climb the summit.

They hadn't seen another car in miles when
Rory started to wriggle in her seat.

"What's the matter?" he asked, not taking his
eyes off the road to look at her. It was always best
to not look at her because doing so messed with
his head in ways he couldn't begin to explain.

"I've got to make a pit stop," she said.

For this he took his gaze off the road and stared
at her in disbelief. "I just asked you if you had to
go. While we were at the damn gas station."

"That was thirty minutes ago. And I didn't have
to go then." She glanced back at Carl. "He has to
go again too."

Bullshit. But as if on cue, Carl whined softly.

Hell. Max gestured to the scene in front of them.
Nothing but thick, unforgiving forestland. "Where
would you like to stop?"

"At a bathroom."

He let out a short laugh. "Okay, princess. I'll just wave my magic wand and make one appear."

She wriggled some more. "Fine. I'll make do. Pull over anywhere, I guess."

"Serious?"

"As a heart attack," she said. "Unless you're not fond of your leather seats?"

He pulled over and together they peered out the windows to the endless sea of woods. "Pick a tree," he said. "Any tree. Make it close to the road because I don't have any snowshoes in the truck."

"I'm not going to pee close to the road."

"Unless you want to wade in up to your cute ass and swim through the accumulation of snow in those woods, that's exactly what you're going to do."

Rory blew out a sigh, zipped up her jacket, and pulled the hood over her head. She opened her door and Carl leapt out ahead of her. She let out a low laugh and then hesitated.

"What?" Max asked.

"Do you think there are bears out there?"

He eyed the foot of fresh snow, still coming down sideways in the vicious wind. "I don't think there's *anything* out there tonight."

"I bet you're just saying that," she said. "You probably *want* a bear to get me."

"I don't want a bear to get you." He didn't. But he wouldn't mind if, say, she stood beneath a tree and it unloaded snow on her . . .

She blinked into the night. "Where did Carl go?"

"Probably to do his business." He hopped out too. "Carl!"

Nothing but the sound of the wind beating up the trees two hundred feet above them. The heavy snow continued to fall but it did so with an eerie, ominous silence.

Shit. "Wait here," he said. "I've got a flashlight in the back."

"I've got a flashlight too—"

"Mine's better."

"How do you know?" she asked, sounding insulted.

"I just do."

"Are you always so obnoxiously stubborn—"

He ignored the rest of that sentence, knowing she couldn't find Carl with the flashlight app on her phone. He dug and came up with his big Maglite, turned back and . . . nearly plowed Rory over because she was standing right there, close, like she'd been snugged up to his back, afraid of the dark. He grabbed her, slipping an arm around her to steady her. "Sorry—"

Sorry nothing. Because she was soft and smelled good and she stood there, right there, with . . . a decent-sized Maglite of her own in one hand, Carl obedient and smiling at her other side.

"Got him," she said sweetly.

Like she was sweet. He knew damn well she was smart as hell, she was resourceful, a survivor . . . She was a *lot* of things, but sweet wasn't one of them.

Then she crouched down and hugged Carl. "Good boy. You were just checking for snakes, weren't you? Such a good, pretty, wonderful boy."

Carl panted happily and set his big head on her shoulder, the ungrateful bastard. They were both covered in snow. Hell, they all were.

While Rory made her way behind a tree, Max dried Carl off and got him into the truck. When Rory came out of the woods, Max really wanted not to care that she was wearing more snow than clothes and shivering, but he couldn't do it. He watched while with shaking hands she carefully shook off before climbing into the truck. Then she stripped out of her jacket that clearly wasn't waterproof.

This left her in a soft off-white sweater that was damp and clinging to her like a second skin. She wore a white lace bra, also damp, and not doing much to hide the fact that she truly was cold. And he was absolutely concentrating on that and how she looked like she needed a hot cheeseburger, and *not* her nipples, two hard little beads threatening to poke through both the lace and the material of her sweater.

Had he thought of her as the sweet, girl-next-door type? Maybe if the girl next door was pinup material, because *damn*. Sitting there with her long waves clinging to her face and shoulders and chest, giving him peekaboo glimpses of her perfect breasts, he couldn't remember why he didn't like her and didn't want to like her.

"What?" she said, wrapping her arms around herself. "You've never seen cold nipples before?"

Yes, but not ones that made his mouth water to taste. Kiss. Nibble. Suck into his mouth . . . "Did you see any bears?"

Rolling her eyes, she pulled a hair tie from around her wrist and used it to contain the wet mass of waves on top of her head.

He handed her a towel, but she shook her head. "I'm fine."

"Yeah, if *fine* is drenched and cold," he said. "Take it. It's not the same one I used on Carl."

"I wouldn't care about that," she said. "But you might have to stop and put on chains soon and you'll need a towel for yourself."

"We're not going to need chains," he said. "I'm in four-wheel drive and we've got good tires. Now use the damn towel, you're dripping all over the place."

As he knew it would, this galvanized her into action and she ran the towel over herself in jerky motions. When she was done, she was still shivering, and after a hesitation, she pulled off her damp sweater.

This left her in a white camisole and aforementioned white lace bra, neither of which were all that significant.

"You going to stare at me all night or get us back on the road?" she asked coolly.

Gentle . . . With that word echoing in his head, he

aimed the heater vents her way and pulled them back onto the highway.

Things had gone downhill in the few minutes they'd been stopped. The snow was really accumulating now, making the highway slick, forcing him to slow down. Way down.

"At this rate, it's gonna take all night to get there," she said, sounding worried.

Most likely she didn't want to spend any more time with him than necessary. But it wasn't like this was how he'd seen himself spending Christmas Eve either.

In the very loud silence of the truck, his belly grumbled, reminding him he'd missed dinner. And lunch. He'd had breakfast but it felt like it'd been days since then.

He heard Rory rustling around and ignored her until a sandwich appeared beneath his nose. "No, thanks," he said.

"*Take it.*"

"I'm good."

"Yeah, well, your stomach says otherwise," she said.

"I'm not eating *your* food," he said, refusing to take the dinner she'd so clearly packed for herself.

She let out a sound of female frustration. "Tell me something. Are you *always* this stubborn or is it something special you save just for me?"

"I meant I'm not eating *your* dinner," he clarified.

"I learned how to share in kindergarten. You should try it sometime."

He blew out a sigh. "Fine. I'll take half if you eat the other half."

She looked surprised and then shrugged. "Deal." Starving to the bone, he wolfed through his portion of her admittedly delicious PB&J and then watched as she ate only half of her half, and then gave the last quarter to Carl.

His heart squeezed as Carl chomped his portion down in one bite, licked his huge chops, and gave her an adoring gaze.

Rory laughed and then pulled something else from her bag of magic tricks—a thermos.

"Hot chocolate," she said, pouring Max half of what she had. "Careful, it's still hot."

"Thanks." He'd known he'd be making this drive tonight and he hadn't given provisions a single thought. After all, he had an emergency kit in the back and he was good.

But she was better. She'd clearly given this lots of thought and was prepared, and it made him wonder why she was going home in the first place. He knew she hadn't been there in years. "I was surprised to find that you were going to Tahoe," he said, fishing.

She sipped her hot chocolate. "Should've packed marshmallows," she murmured.

He had the oddest urge to stop and get her some but they were nowhere near a store.

She drained her cup and had a chocolate mustache. Her tongue came out and licked her lips with great relish and he nearly ran them off the road.

Startled, she glanced over at him.

He stared resolutely straight ahead at the road—or what he could see of it—wondering what the hell this odd reaction to her was. Uncalled for. Stupid. *Very* stupid.

"You okay?" she asked.

"Terrific. You didn't answer my question."

"You didn't ask one."

He resisted rolling his eyes. "Why are you going home this year?"

She shrugged. "My family and I have a rocky relationship. Mostly because I've flaked on them, a lot. I'm . . . undependable. I wanted to change that." She paused. "If I can."

Max thought of the life she led now, going to school, working hard. "You seem pretty dependable to me."

"Yes, well, thankfully things change. People change." She hesitated again, and he realized she was weighing how much she wanted to tell him. "I'm not sure my family gets that," she finally said. "I've let them down."

He was sympathetic to that. He'd been a punk-ass teenager himself. If his family judged him off that asshole he'd once been, they wouldn't like him very much either. "Then and now are different," he said. "They'll see that."

She didn't look convinced and he couldn't blame

her. Because even *he'd* been judging her off some-thing she'd done in the past. Which made him a first-class jerk.

"You do realize the gas pedal is the narrow one on the right," she said.

He glanced over at her. "Excuse me?"

"You're driving like a granny without her spec-tacles, and I'm in a time crunch."

He choked out a laugh. "In case you haven't no-ticed, things are a little dicey out there."

She shrugged, unimpressed. "We've both seen worse."

True enough. But she was also deflecting and trying to change the subject. "You left home hard and fast years ago and never looked back. So I don't get it, Rory. What's your sudden rush?"

She looked away. "It's a long story."

"And?"

"And trust me, we don't have enough time."

Before he could react to that, he saw the block-ades ahead. "Shit," he said. "Highway's closed."

The flashing sign said there'd been an accident ahead and to please be patient. Ha. Easy enough for the damn sign to say; it wasn't stuck in a car with a woman he couldn't figure out whether he wanted to strangle or kiss.

"Looks like we've suddenly got plenty of time," he said, wondering if she'd talk to him now, sur-prised at how much he wanted her to. Because in spite of himself, he was fascinated and drawn to *this* Rory, the sexy, smart, resourceful woman sitting next to him. When she didn't respond, he glanced over at her, startled to find her pale, her eyes suspiciously wet. "What?" he asked, whipping his head around to see what had happened, where the big bad was coming from, but he couldn't see a problem. "What is it?"

She just shook her head and began to rifle through her bag, keeping her face averted.

Tears? What had caused such a strong emotion? Clueless and hating that, Max reached down and pulled out a few napkins he kept shoved into the door pouch for those days when he was chowing down a burger and driving at the same time. "Here," he said, and thrust them at her.

She took them without a word and blew her nose. "Thanks," she finally said. "I, um, had something in my eye."

She was talking to her passenger window. Reaching out, he touched her to get her to turn toward him, finding himself stunned when he connected with the bare skin of her arm and felt a zip of electrical current that wasn't electricity at all, but sheer chemistry. "Rory," he said, hardly recognizing his own voice, it was so low and rough.

She stared at him and then her gaze dropped to his mouth and he had one thought—ah, hell, he was in trouble. Deep trouble.

The next girl you feel something for, anything at all, you have to go for it, no exceptions . . .

He had laughed at Cass's words, secure in the

knowledge there wasn't anyone in his life to feel something for right now. Or at least no one he *wanted* to feel something for.

But that was starting to change, right before his very eyes.

Chapter Four

Rory couldn't believe how difficult it was to stop staring at Max's mouth, or to force herself to lift her gaze to his eyes.

Eyes that were dark. Deep. Unfathomable.

He was waiting on an answer. But there was no way she would admit the truth to him, that she felt compelled to get home with her stepdad's gift for her mom by dawn when they opened presents or she wouldn't be forgiven. "I've changed my mind," she said. "It's not a story I'm willing to tell no matter how much time we have."

"Because it makes you cry?" he asked.

"I wasn't crying," she said. "I don't cry."

He arched a brow her way. "Ever?"

"Ever." She narrowed her eyes. "Why, do you?"

"Sure," he said with an easy shrug of his wide shoulders.

Sure. Like it was the most natural thing in the world to feel so strongly about something that it made you cry. She let out a low, disbelieving laugh. "When?" she asked. "*When* was the last time you cried?"

Max appeared to give this some serious thought. "When I watched *The Good Dinosaur* with my niece last month," he said. "Bawled like a baby." He smiled. "She did too."

Huh. Maybe he was human after all. "Was it the scene where Disney slayed us all through the heart by killing the dad?" she asked. "Or when Spot showed us how he lost his family?"

"Neither," he said. "It happened when my niece ate my ice cream."

She rolled her eyes and turned back to the window.

"Hey," he said, "it was traumatic."

She snorted. "Do you even know the definition of *traumatic*?"

He slid her a look and then gave his attention back to the road, even though they were at a dead stop. "I do," he said.

"Really? You of the perfect family and college basketball scholarship to Michigan State and—"

His head whipped back to hers, his expression dark and incredulous.

Accusatory.

"You know what that thing with Cindy cost me," he finally said. "And I'm over it, long over it, but you can add it to the list of things we're not discussing. Not that and not your part in it, because back then I had no choice but to believe you were the kind of person willing to hurt whoever you had to in order to win. I can concede that maybe you've changed, but history can't be rewritten."

She stared at him, stunned. Cindy had been a classmate who'd taken great pleasure in being as cruel and horrible to Rory as possible. She'd been popular, a great athlete, a great student, and the daughter of the basketball coach. Every guy in the school had crushed on her and she could've had any one of them.

So of course she'd taken the only guy Rory had ever wanted.

Max.

Cindy had been one of those sweet on the outside, toxic on the inside people who were so scary to Rory. It'd been Cindy who in their junior year had lied to their teacher and gotten Rory suspended for cheating when it had been Cindy who'd cheated. Then she'd stolen Rory's clothes from her locker during PE class and had sneakily taken a pic of Rory in her underwear. Cindy had texted it to everyone in school—from Rory's own phone. Just remembering it had her cheeks heating. Her mom and stepdad had been furious at her for all of it, the supposed cheating and the picture. Rory had been devastated and needing sympathy on that in a very bad way, but instead they'd grounded her because they'd actually believed she'd sent that pic herself.

When someone had begun letting themselves into the coach's office to have sex, Cindy started a rumor that it was Rory, all to deflect blame from herself. After all, it wouldn't look good for the sweet, wonderful, lovable coach's daughter to be caught doing it in daddy's office.

Facing expulsion only a week before finals, Rory had finally resorted to taping Cindy leaving her dad's office with a guy in hand. The guy had been in shadow, but there'd been no doubt, at least to her, that it'd been Max.

Yeah, her bad, but she'd had to prove herself innocent. And besides, no one else had seemed to know it was him so she had no idea why he was so pissed. She would ask him but the truth was that she was embarrassed. *Deeply* embarrassed. She wasn't proud of what she'd done. In her mind, the minute she'd turned the tape into the school proving she hadn't been the one breaking into the coach's office, she'd gone from being The Bullied to The Bullier, and she'd hated herself for that.

So much so that she'd left town.

She'd been planning on leaving for a long time anyway. With her mom remarried and having three new kids, it'd been one less mouth to feed, so she'd taken a bus to San Francisco.

Relatively speaking, she'd been one of the lucky runaways. After an admittedly very rough start, she'd taken a part-time job at South Bark, where Willa had tucked her under her wing, teaching her the business and making her take her GED, and in the process had given her back a life that could so easily have gone wrong.

In any case, she was no longer that same Rory she'd once been. When Max had started working in the same building as her last year, she'd been so nervous he'd want to talk about that time in their lives, the time she'd been so very miserable and unhappy.

She had been so relieved when he hadn't seemed to want to talk at all.

But now she realized they should have. Because he was over there on his side of the truck emitting animosity in waves and insinuating that she'd cost him something big.

Not that he appeared at all interested in enlightening her on what.

Fine. She could read between the lines somewhat and she'd get to the bottom of this in her usual way—on her own. For now, he'd turned off the engine to preserve gas, and now it was cold and quickly getting colder. She pulled a blanket from her bag.

He snorted but when she looked at him, he was staring out the windshield, jaw tight, eyes hard, one hand draped over the wheel, the other fisted on a thigh. She figured he was made of stone but she lifted up one end of her blanket in offer. "Cold?" she asked.

"No."

Sensing the thick tension, Carl whined softly.

Rory reached out to test-touch Max's hand.

Cold.

"Seriously?" she asked him and spread half the blanket over his legs.

He didn't help her but when she was finished, she found him staring at her like she was a puzzle and he was missing half the pieces.

But *she* was the one who didn't understand. And she was done not knowing. "So," she said tentatively. "You didn't take your scholarship?"

He closed his eyes for a beat and shook his head. "Why do you keep saying things like that when you know damn well what happened?"

Okay so no, he hadn't taken the scholarship, and she got a feeling in the pit of her stomach that she'd been the direct cause.

Carl whined again.

"Forget it," Max told him. "I'm not letting you out again."

"Max," she said. "I—"

"Finally." He pointed ahead, where the blockades were being removed.

Max cranked over the engine and rolled his window down when a CHP officer came close.

"Don't know how long we'll have the roads open," the guy told them. "It's looking grim."

"Thanks," Max said. "We'll be careful."

And he was. So careful it felt like they were going backward. Rory looked at her phone.

No reception, which meant she couldn't call her stepdad and warn him she'd be late. It was still snowing, it was tense, there was no one else on the road . . . All that, along with the rhythmic slashing of the windshield wipers and the soft blast of the heater left her feeling exhausted. She closed her eyes.

And then jerked upright when the truck slowed and then came to a stop off the side of the road.

She wasn't sure how much time had passed. The snow had been steadily gathering, over a foot now, she saw with some alarm. They'd pulled up behind a small SUV that was leaning awkwardly due to a blown tire.

"Stay here," Max said.

"What are you doing?" she asked.

He spared her a look as he pulled up his hoodie. "Going to help them out."

He said it like it was his problem the SUV was in trouble. Like he could no more pass another car in need of assistance than he could stop inhaling and exhaling air for his lungs.

"But—" she started. But nothing, because he was already gone. She watched him trudge through the snow, lit by his high beams, toward the other SUV.

Two people got out to greet him, an older couple by the looks of them. They spoke to Max, who nodded. Even smiled. He said something to the older man, patted the woman reassuringly on the arm and . . . went to the back of his truck, probably for tools.

"He's going to say he doesn't need anything from me," she said to Carl. "But we're going to offer to help anyway." She pulled her wet sweater and jacket back on and slid out of the truck, smiling at the couple. She moved toward Max, on his knees in the snow now, wrenching off the bad tire with easy strength and ability.

He could be *such* an ass. But he was also selfless. Kind. Funny. Well, at least with everyone else anyway.

The older woman smiled and shook her head at Rory. "We're so grateful that you stopped. We've been here for an hour with no cell service. We couldn't call for help. Our kids and grandkids will be so worried."

Rory managed a smile around a suddenly tight throat. Would her family be worried? Or would they just assume she'd flaked yet again? "You have a big family?"

"You might say so." The woman laughed. "Six kids. Twelve grandkids." She laughed again at the look on Rory's face. "We've been together since the dawn of time, you see." She looked toward the men, shaking hands now since Max was already finished, and beamed. "And after all these years, he still makes my heart flutter."

"That's incredibly sweet," Rory said.

The older woman squeezed her hand. "Whatever you two are arguing about, my dear, you can work it out."

Rory looked at her, startled. "How do you know we're arguing?"

"Since the dawn of time, remember? I know the signs." She smiled. "Would you like a hint on how to fix it?"

Rory looked into her kind eyes. "Yes, please."

"You use the past to fix the now," she said. "You make your mistakes—which is allowed, by the way. After all, you're only human, but you learn from them. Grow from them. Things can't always be forgotten, but they can be forgiven."

Rory turned to look at Max. She'd most definitely learned from her mistakes. Grown from them. But . . . had she been forgiven for them?

The old couple got into their SUV and drove off. Rory helped Max gather the few tools he'd used.

"Get in the truck," he said. "I've got this."

She stubbornly went to the back of the truck with him to put the tools away. They both leaned in, reaching out to close the toolbox at the same time, their faces close, their hands colliding. She took in the scent of him, some sort of innately sexy guy soap. He hadn't shaved that morning and the sight of the stubble on his strong jaw had a funny slide going through her belly.

Suddenly he appeared to realize how close their faces were and jerked back. "Get out of the snow," he said.

He was just as covered in it as she. In fact, every inch of his jacket was layered in fresh powder. "Right back at you," she said.

Reaching out, he ran a hand over her head and shoulders, brushing snow from her, an action that had the quiver in her belly heading south.

She didn't want to feel anything for him, she really didn't, but she couldn't seem to stop herself. A low sound that came horrifying close to a moan escaped her and Max stilled.

God. He'd heard and now her humiliation was complete—

"Get in the truck and out of this weather," he repeated, his voice still low and rough but somehow softer. *"Please."*

She drew in a surprised breath at that. She wasn't used to the "please," not from him anyway. She nodded and left him alone.

Two minutes later he'd joined her and Carl in the truck and . . .

The engine wouldn't start.

Chapter Five

"Sʜɪᴛ," Mᴀx said after a few more tries. He leaned back, frustration in every line of his body.

"What's wrong?" Rory asked, afraid she already knew.

"Dead battery." He shook his head. "I was going to give the truck an overhaul this week with my dad and that's one of the things I was going to replace. I think the frigid temps finished her off."

Rory looked at the time. Eleven thirty. On Christmas Eve, no less. Not good, not good at all, but she tried not to panic.

And failed miserably.

"So . . . what now?" she asked in what she hoped was a casual voice.

He glanced over at her as if maybe she'd given away her panic regardless. He pulled out his phone and looked at the screen. "Still no cell service," he said in disgust. "I'm going to have to flag someone down for a jump-start."

She had no idea how long that would take but it surely wasn't going to be quick and her heart sank.

Getting home by dawn wasn't looking good, but surely *someone* would stop. She looked out into the night.

Not another vehicle in sight.

It was like they were on Mars.

Use the past to fix the now . . . The woman's words floated around in her head and it came to her that maybe this trip could be about more than just making up with her family. She could make up with Max. If he'd let her. "Max?"

"Yeah?"

"Did Cindy break up with you after I turned in the video?" she asked. "Is that why you're mad at me?"

Max leaned forward and knocked his head against his steering wheel several times.

"Look," she said softly. "I'm sorry. And I should've said that a long time ago. The video . . . it wasn't about you—"

Head still down, he snorted.

"It wasn't," she insisted.

Max shook his head, straightened, and slid out of the truck.

No doubt to get away from her.

Standing there in the glare of the headlights, legs spread, feet solidly planted against the wind and snow, he looked tough as hell.

But so was she, she reminded herself.

So she got out and stood next to him.

"What are you doing?" He had to raise his voice to be heard over the wind. "Get back inside."

She couldn't. She had to know; it was killing her. "What did I cost you, Max?"

He shoved his hands into his pockets. He was watching the highway, clearly willing a car to come along that he could flag down. But there was no one but her.

"Max, please," she said. "Just tell me."

He inhaled deeply. "Cindy got suspended," he said. "A hand slap, considering. They didn't know it was me in the tape but I had to—" He shook his head. "We'd already moved on from each other but I still couldn't not say anything . . . "

She wasn't going to like this story, she could tell. "You came forward," she guessed.

He shrugged, like there'd been no other option.

How had she not seen that coming? No way would a guy like Max let a girl take all the blame for something he'd been involved in as well.

"And then I was suspended too," he said.

"Oh, Max," she breathed. "I'm so sorry."

He turned to her then, his eyes hard. "It wasn't the suspension that got me. Hell, I deserved it. I did it. I was there and I knew we shouldn't be and I'm just lucky I wasn't expelled. But Coach . . . he was royally pissed off and looking for blood. He cut me from the team for misconduct, which broke the verbal contract I had to go play for Michigan State. They dumped me."

She stared at him in horror. "But you were so good," she said. "Why didn't someone else pick you up?"

"Most teams were already full. After I graduated, I could've walked on somewhere and tried out, but we couldn't afford for me to go anywhere without a guaranteed scholarship. So I didn't."

She told herself it was the wind and icy cold stinging her eyes. "Max, I—"

"If you're about to say you're sorry, save it."

"But—"

"Someone's coming," he said, eyes sharp on the road. "Get back in the truck—"

"Max—"

"Dammit, Rory, this isn't exactly safe, okay? We're out on the highway, fairly defenseless. I want you locked in the truck until I see who stops for us."

Okay, she got that, but she hated the idea of him being out here on his own.

He laughed a little harshly, as if reading her thoughts. "I might not have ended up with a degree but trust me, princess, I'm qualified for this."

"Call me princess one more time and I'll—"

"*Truck,*" he said tightly.

Getting that she was a liability at the moment, she did as he'd asked and got into the truck.

Which was when she realized it was empty of one oversized Doberman. "Carl?"

Nothing.

Where the hell had he gone? Realizing he must have escaped when she'd gotten out, she whirled back around to get her eyes on Max. She watched him step closer to the approaching car but not too close, bending down a little to peek into the passenger window when it slid down only a few inches.

He looked like quite the imposing figure, tall, built, fiercely serious in the moment, and she wondered what they were talking about.

Then he turned his head and looked right at her through the windshield and she knew. They were talking about her.

Max nodded to the person in the car and then he strode through the driving snow toward her.

"Max," she said immediately when he came around, not to the driver's side but to her passenger side and opened the door. "Carl's gone."

He stood there in the vee of space between the door and the body of the truck, sheltering her from the worst of the storm. "He probably went into the woods to do his business. He'll be right back. About the car—"

"Are they going to help?" she asked.

"It's a guy in a big hurry to get to his wife," he said. "She's in labor at the hospital in Tahoe. He promised to call for a tow truck as soon as he got over the summit and got any reception."

"Do you think he will?"

Max shrugged. "I hope so. I know him, or I know who he is. He works with my older sister at the post office. He's a good guy, married with three other kids. He says you can hitch a ride with him so you won't miss Christmas morning. But you have to decide right this minute. He's out of time."

If she went, she could get home by dawn and

make amends with her family. It was perfect and she was grateful for the offer but—

Max, apparently taking her silence as a yes, reached in to take her hand.

"No," she said, resisting but not letting go of his hand. Her heart was pounding. She knew she should take this opportunity and go. That's what this whole thing was all about—getting home in time. Or that's what she thought it'd been all about.

But in that moment, she knew it was about far more. Like being a better person, one who put others first.

"No?" he repeated.

"No. Thank you but no. I'm not going when you're stranded here with Carl missing."

"I'll find Carl," he said.

"You might need help," she insisted. "I'm not leaving you."

He stared at her in disbelief. "Rory, I can handle this."

"Maybe." Okay, definitely. Not the point. She wasn't walking away from a friend. And yeah, maybe at the moment they weren't friends exactly, but they were . . . *something.* "I'm still not leaving you out here alone in this storm on the side of the road," she said. "So tell him thank you and good luck to him and his wife but I'm staying with you."

Max looked at her as if she'd lost her damn mind but he strode back to the car, said a few words, and then the car was gone, leaving them alone on top of the world in a massive blizzard.

Max whistled for Carl but the wind was so loud, the sound got swallowed up.

Rory slipped out of the truck and back into the mind-numbing cold to make her way to Max. "Carl!" she yelled and nearly got blown over by the next gust of wind.

Max caught her and held her at his side. "You could've gotten home," he said. "You know you're crazy, right?" he asked.

Yes, she knew. And yeah, her whole purpose had been to show her family she'd changed but hey, there'd be plenty of time to stress about that later. "This is for Carl, not you."

He choked out a rough laugh. "You're still crazy," he said but he'd kept his arm around her, holding her close. And he didn't sound quite as mad at her anymore.

Which might have just been wishful thinking on her part.

"Carl!" Max yelled, using the hand that wasn't holding onto her to cup around his mouth. "Carl, *come!*"

From out of the woods came a huge snow abomination. When it was only a few feet from them, it stopped, shook, and sent snow flying.

Carl.

Proud of himself, he sat happily at their feet and panted a smile, while Rory fought with relieved tears.

What was wrong with her tonight?

Max got them all back into the truck. He dried

off Carl the best he could and then turned to Rory.

She had no idea that she'd lost the battle with her emotions until Max cupped her face and swiped a tear from her cheek with his thumb. "Rory," he said, voice low and concerned.

"Does Christmas always have to suck so hard?" she whispered.

He looked at her for a long beat and then slowly shook his head. "No. Not always."

They stared at each other some more and then . . . he kissed her. Softly at first, carefully, but she didn't need either and let him know by fisting her hands in his jacket and letting out a needy little whimper for more.

This wrenched a deep, rough male groan from him that rumbled up from his chest, and she clutched at him, trying to get closer. Before she knew it, he'd hauled her over the console and into his lap, tucking her thighs on either side of his, letting her feel *exactly* how his body had responded to the kiss. He was hard.

Everywhere.

Hungry for the connection, desperate to forget her problems, trembling in her boots for more of this man beneath her, she kissed him back with all the pent-up longing and need she felt. When they broke free, his eyes were heavy-lidded with lust and desire, and she had one single, devastating thought.

All these years later, she still wanted him as her own.

Chapter Six

MAX DIDN'T often act without deliberate conscious thought. In his job, his life depended on him being a clear, levelheaded thinker at all times.

But at the moment, with the wind and snow beating up his truck on the outside, the interior both dark and intimate, his tongue halfway down Rory's throat, he couldn't kick-start his brain or mobilize his thoughts. All he could do was feel. And, Christ, what he felt. Rory's loose hair streaming over his shoulders and arms as she strained against him, her petite body chilled enough to sink in and concern him—which was an excuse to wrap her up even tighter in his arms.

Better.

Carl gave a happy "wuff," and clearly thinking they were *all* going to wrestle, he tried to stick his big, fat head in between them.

Rory choked out a laugh and gave the dog a playful shove and then, in what might have been Max's favorite part of the day, hell his entire year, Rory slid her fingers back into his hair and kissed *him*.

Yeah, that worked. Big time. He tried to keep it

light but she kept responding with more than he expected, sweeping her tongue into his mouth, sliding it sensually against his, and he was a goner. With a groan, he tightened his grip on her and gave her all he had.

She whispered his name, her voice filled with such longing that it reached deep inside his chest and squeezed around his heart. She was still straddling him, her knees tucked on either side of his hips, and then she rocked against his killer hard-on and he forgot to breathe. But breathing was optional anyway as he kissed her hungrily, completely lost in her, just gone.

When she finally pulled free, she was breathless, her eyes dazed, her lips full and wet. "What was that for?" she asked softly.

He had no idea. She was driving him crazy. Since the day he'd begun working in the same building as her and he'd realized that there was a serious chemistry between them, she'd been driving him crazy. But this was a whole new level of crazy, the kind that made him want to get her naked so he could warm her up in the most basic of ways.

Not good.

None of this was good, this seeing new sides of her that he didn't want to see. Rory sharing everything she had, Rory being sweet and kind. Resourceful. And incredibly courageous. And, Christ, but he really loved that about her. She'd been through hell and was here on the other side, stronger than ever.

The thing was, in his life, he took care of people. Clients at work. Coworkers. Carl. His friends. His family. Although . . . it hadn't escaped him who'd been taking care of who on this trip.

"Max?"

"I don't know what that was," he said. "You turn me upside down."

She let out a snort. Clearly he wasn't the only one off his axis.

Headlights came up behind them, uncomfortably close. All he could see in the dark night was that the vehicle was large. Possibly a tow truck, *hopefully* a tow truck but possibly not, and he carefully nudged Rory off his lap and back to her seat. Her eyes widened when he leaned forward to grab the Maglite he'd left at his feet and his jacket raised up, clearly revealing the gun at the small of his back.

"What—"

"Wait here," he said, and then he slid out of the truck, locking it behind him. They were on a deserted road in a damn blizzard.

Sitting ducks.

But it was a tow truck. "Got a call," the driver said, hopping out. "Bad battery?"

"Yeah, if you can just give me a jump, I should be able to get it home and replace it."

The guy nodded and they went to work.

"Hopefully you get all the way through," the tow truck driver said when they had Max's truck running again. "I heard they're going to close the road five miles up. There's a wreck that they might not get cleared until morning."

Hell. "Thanks." He got back into his truck and looked at Rory. And Carl too, since he was once again in her lap, the big baby. Max didn't feel like smiling but that's exactly what he did since his dog was bigger than she was. "Shouldn't *you* be in *his* lap?"

She had her arms wrapped around Carl in a hug and they looked pretty comfy. "He wanted a snuggle."

No shit. Any male in his right mind would want a snuggle from Rory. The thought surprised him. But it was the utter truth. "We can go back," he said, "or we can forge forward with no guarantee. What's your vote?"

She looked surprised. "You're giving me a say?"

"Yes," he said. "Merry Christmas."

She rolled her eyes but stared at him some more, her expression going solemn and serious. Whatever her thoughts, they were deep and troubled, and he knew it was related to why she was in such a desperate hurry to get home.

"I vote forge forward," she finally said.

He nodded. "Forward it is then."

But three minutes later he was second-guessing their decision. The snow had gotten worse and so had the driving conditions.

"I get why you're mad at me," Rory said quietly. "And I know it won't help anything, but . . . "

"I don't need an apology from you," he said. He felt her gaze on him but kept his on the road. "*Shit*."

"What?"

He pointed to the flashing sign ahead: *Highway closed three miles ahead.*

Take next exit to turn around.

She didn't speak, but her sucked in gasp spoke volumes. They were silent as he got off at the exit. They were in a very small mountain town. Actually *town* might be a bit overstated. There was a gas station, a convenience store, and a tiny motel. Emphasis on *tiny*.

Max pulled into the lot. "I'm going to ask you one more time—go back or stay and get rooms?"

She bit her lower lip.

"It's one in the morning," he said. "I'm exhausted. You look exhausted."

Carl let out a low huff.

"And Carl's exhausted," he added and got a ghost of a smile from Rory. "If we get rooms, we would get some sleep and hopefully the roads will open up at daylight."

"Daylight," she repeated softly, staring out the window. "So we won't make it home by dawn."

There was something in her voice. Emotion. Deep emotion. "Better than going back to San Francisco though, right?" he asked.

She didn't answer.

"Rory? Stay or go?"

She closed her eyes. "Stay."

"Okay." He nodded. "Do you want to call home? I'm sure there's a phone in there we can use."

"It's too late," she said softly. "They go to bed early. It's okay, I'll call them in the morning. I don't want to wake up the whole house."

"Okay. Wait here with Carl for a sec, I've gotta go try to bribe them into letting him stay as well, otherwise I'm stuck in the truck."

"*We're* stuck in the truck," she said, reaching to pet Carl.

We. Shit. He hoped to God he had enough cash on him to bribe whoever was in that motel, because the close quarters inside the truck would kill him long before dawn.

Chapter Seven

Max didn't wait for an answer; he just slid out of the truck and strode purposefully toward the small motel. Rory watched him go, his gait confident, those broad shoulders squared against the wind.

"He never second-guesses himself, does he?" she murmured to Carl, her own shoulders slumping.

Carl, who'd climbed into the driver's seat the second Max had vacated it, licked her chin.

"He's also still not thrilled with me, kiss or no," she said.

Carl whined and sniffed at her bag, probably hungry for another PB&J.

"At least it finally makes sense now, given what I cost him." She sighed. "I really blew it, Carl."

He whined again and bumped his face to hers. She hugged him tight, burying her face in the short but soft fur at his neck. "I knew you'd forgive me."

Back then she'd really believed turning in the video had been a victory. Her first. She'd actually won at something, gotten the upper hand.

But she'd been wrong. It'd been a terribly selfish thing to do, leaving Max to pay the price, and what was worse, she hadn't even realized it because she'd been blinded by her need for revenge.

She really hated that.

She startled when Max opened the door and wind and snow blew in. "Let's go," he said.

"They'll take Carl?"

"Had to pay double, but yeah." He grabbed their two bags and tossed her the leash. "You got him?"

For some reason that made her feel slightly better. Though he had good reason to hate her, he didn't, not if he trusted her with Carl. Maybe he'd finally really hear her apology. "Max?"

He turned to her, impatience on his face. There were snowflakes clinging to his perfectly long, inky black eyelashes, and his jaw was tight.

She bit her lower lip. "I just want to say how sorry I am that—"

"Not now."

"Then when?"

His laugh was humorless. "Rory, it's ten fucking degrees and it's coming down sideways out here. You're shaking so hard your teeth are going to rattle out of your mouth."

"I don't care." She reached out and grabbed a fistful of his jacket to hold him still. "I'm trying to make everything okay, Max. Don't you get it? I really *need* everything to be okay. God, just once in my life, I need that. I can't live with all this past stuff in my head anymore, I'm going to lose my mind." She gripped his jacket tighter and put her face in his. "So I'm going to tell you I'm sorry and you're going to listen to me, dammit!"

He hadn't so much as blinked as she basically yelled at him but she thought maybe there was the slightest softening in his hard eyes. "Okay," he said.

"Okay." She let out a breath and nodded. "Good."

"You ready to go inside now or do you need to yell at me some more?" he asked.

She choked out a laugh and got out of the truck.

The lobby of the motel consisted of a desk and a love seat that looked like it'd seen better days. So did the paint on the walls and the floors. The wide-screen TV though, that was brand spanking new and the twentysomething guy in front of it waved them through a hallway without taking his eyes off his show. "Last two rooms on the right," he said, glancing over, his gaze slowing a little as he took in Rory. "They connect if you want them to," he added slyly.

Rory stumbled but Max caught her and nudged her along without comment.

To their connecting rooms.

She didn't say a word as they stopped in front of the first door. Max handed her a key and waited until she unlocked it.

"Try to get some sleep," he said. "I'll come for you when the roads are open and clear."

"You kissed me."

"Yeah."

"You kissed me like you *liked* me," she said.

He just held her gaze as snow flew all around them.

She drew a deep breath. "Max, the girl who made that video, she isn't the same woman standing here in front of you. You have to know that."

Max dropped his head and stared at his boots for a beat before meeting her gaze again. "Look, maybe we could go in our rooms and take showers to recover from the snow apocalypse, and then take some time to think things through like rational people. Would that work for you?"

She paused and then nodded.

A very slight bit of humor came into his gaze. "You sure?" he asked. "Because if you want to go back outside in this crazy-ass storm and yell at me on Christmas Eve some more, that works too."

She rolled her eyes and turned back to her door. "The rooms connect."

"Yes."

She glanced at him. "You going to knock first?"

He studied her for a long moment and then stepped into her a little bit, enough to make her breathing hitch and her heart skip a beat. His fingers stroked a rogue strand of hair from her temple. "Worried?"

Yes. She was worried that he *wouldn't* come over at all.

"Listen," he said. "Let it all go for tonight, okay?

I mean what's the worst that could happen—you wake up and go back to worrying in the morning? Because maybe life'll surprise you and everything'll be fine."

She gave a rough laugh and he smiled. "It could happen," he said.

"Not in my world."

His smile faded. "There's a first time for everything, Rory. Shut and lock the door. You know where to find me if you need me."

He said this lightly but she had a feeling he was hoping she wouldn't need him. Which was fine. She didn't need anyone, thank you very much. So she did as he said. She shut and locked her door and stared at the small but neat room. She set down her duffel bag and then eyeballed the connecting door to Max's room.

The walls were thin. She could hear him unlocking his door and then the padding of Carl as he trotted in.

"Stop," Max said and Rory froze.

"Don't drool on the windows."

Rory had to laugh at herself and then imagined Carl at the window, up on his back legs so he could see out into the night.

"You wouldn't believe the security deposit I had to put down for you," Max said, tone warning, "and I want it back, every penny."

There was a thump. Probably Max's duffel bag hitting the floor. And then the interior door, her connecting door, rattled a tiny bit.

He'd unlocked his connecting door, she realized as her heart took a good solid leap.

He wanted her to be able to get him if she needed him.

"Don't even think about the bed," Max said. "I've got dibs. I'm taking a quick shower first. Don't eat anything while I'm gone, you hear me?"

There was a silence and then the sound of a door shutting and water coming on.

Max in the shower.

A thought that gave Rory a hot flash. The guy went to the gym. He ran. He kicked ass at work. He was all solid, lean muscle, and knowing he was stripping down and stepping into a steamy hot shower had her pulse rate in overdrive.

She tried to remind herself that he didn't like her very much but she had to admit, his actions toward her didn't support that theory. He'd given her a ride. He'd looked out for her, finding her an alternate ride when his truck had failed them. He'd gotten her a motel room. He'd been protective, if not exactly the "gentle" that Willa had asked him for, and he'd certainly been kind.

And then there'd been the kiss that had led to a make-out session for the record books. Just thinking about it had her nipples hard again and started that tingle in her thighs.

She liked him, she *really* liked him.

And she always had.

"Dammit," she whispered.

Get some sleep, he'd said. But she knew she wouldn't. She couldn't.

She'd cost him a scholarship.

She'd ruined his life.

No, she wouldn't sleep. Not until she knew she'd done her best to make things right.

Chapter Eight

Max stood in the shower, hands flat on the tile wall, his head bent so that the hot water could beat down on him.

My family and I have a rocky relationship. I've flaked on them, a lot. I'm . . . undependable. I wanted to change that this year . . .

It pissed him off that Rory's family didn't see her for the incredible woman she was. She deserved support from them. Shaking his head, he turned off the water and grabbed a towel.

I'm still not leaving you out here alone in this storm on the side of the road . . .

He still couldn't believe how amazingly fierce she'd been, standing there in the crazy storm, teeth chattering and still, refusing to leave him alone.

Not the sign of a flaky woman, one who didn't care about anyone other than herself. In fact, she was the exact opposite of that.

Running the towel over his wet head, he stepped out of the bathroom and heard a sharp gasp.

Definitely not Carl.

Lifting his head, he met Rory's shocked gaze as it ran down the length of his nude body.

"Um," she said.

He arched a brow. "Didn't hear you knock."

"Um," she said again but didn't, he couldn't help but notice, look away.

He walked to the duffel bag on the floor, squatted low, and rifled through for a clean pair of jeans. Straightening, he pulled them on and turned back to her.

She blinked. "You're . . . commando."

"And you found your words again."

She rolled her eyes so hard he was surprised they didn't come out of the sockets. "I'm just discombobulated because we didn't get home," she said just defensively enough to make him grin.

"And here I thought it was me naked."

"Fine," she said, blushing. "Maybe it was a little bit you naked."

"Yeah, if you could not use 'little' and 'naked' in the same sentence about me," he said and smiled when she found a laugh.

"Okay, I want to start over." She took a deep breath. "I cost you your college education."

He shook his head. "I shouldn't have told you that."

"Yes, you should have. I still can't believe I didn't know." She shook her head, looking devastated. "No wonder you hated me all this time, and now you're stuck with me on Christmas Eve and I don't even have a present to give you in the morning."

He choked out a low laugh. "I never hated you, Rory."

A lot crossed her face at that. Hope. Relief. "No?"

"No." He hesitated, something he rarely did. "Look, if we're sharing and all that, then there's some things you should know."

Her gaze locked on his and held. "Like?"

He sighed. "It's true that back then I was pissed off. I was angry at the world, actually, and also going out with girls I wouldn't look twice at now because I was a first-class ass, but I'm glad it all happened the way it did. I wouldn't change it."

"You wouldn't?" she asked, her fingers tightly entwined together, knuckles white.

Shaking his head, he stepped toward her and took her hands in his, gently applying pressure until she loosened her fingers so he could clasp them in his. "I'd have ended up in Michigan," he said. "It's fucking cold in Michigan."

She snorted. "It's fucking cold *here*."

He smiled and shook his head. "Not in this room it's not."

She caught her lower lip between her teeth. "Max—"

"My point is that I love San Francisco," he said. "I love my job, my place, my friends. My life there is good. Great, actually."

She let out a long, shaky breath. "Thanks. You didn't have to say that."

"Yeah," he said, letting his hands come up to her arms. "I did."

She met his gaze, her own honest and earnest and remorseful. "I really am so very sorry. What I did was selfish, and worse, I never even gave a second thought to the mess I left you in. It was all about me trying to get revenge on Cindy, but you got screwed over so much more than she did."

True. He'd been dumped by his very angry coach, humiliated in front of the entire town, and his family had been shocked and disappointed in him. He hadn't gotten over it for a damn long time, certainly much longer than anyone cared about the damn video. And he'd been confused too, because he'd liked Rory. She'd been quiet but nice. And funny. He'd never seen her as one of the mean girls. "Why did you do it?" he asked. "What did you mean, you wanted revenge on Cindy?"

She gave him a questioning look. "You knew that she accused me of being the one to break into her dad's office. She said that she'd seen me do it, that I was the one stealing money from the coaches' bags, among other things."

"No," Max said slowly. "I didn't know that."

"When I actually caught her at it, she turned it around on me," she said softly, her eyes on his. "I was suspended."

"I knew you'd been suspended for stealing something from the school but I didn't know what."

She shook her head. "I didn't steal anything. And she kept getting me in trouble, one thing after another, making things up so I came off as unreliable in case I tried to turn her in."

"I'm sorry," he said. "I'd like to say I dumped her for being a bitch but the fact is, I didn't care what she was like. You should have turned her in regardless."

She just looked at him.

"Oh." He let out a low laugh. "Right. You did. You videoed her and got me as well."

"A mistake," she said. "You were collateral damage, and I'm so very sorry, Max."

He got that. He appreciated that. But the past was the past and he had some things to say too. "Listen, I was a teenage jerk and I thought the world revolved around me. It never occurred to me that you were in trouble, that you weren't even targeting me. I was *that* self-absorbed, and I hate that."

She started to shake her head and say something more but he covered her lips with a finger. He needed to finish, to get this out, because he was realizing a couple of things. He'd wronged her in much the same way everyone else in her life had, and that was a hard pill to swallow because he prided himself on always trying to do the right thing. "You're done apologizing to me," he said. "I was a complete dick about it earlier, but I was wrong. Then and now."

"Max—"

He applied gentle pressure on her mouth. "There's nothing to forgive, okay? You were only doing what you had to to get through and I get it. Now it's my turn to apologize to you."

This startled her into silence. He smiled, his fingers stroking her jaw while his thumb rasped over her lower lip. "I should have listened to you. But also I should've known there was more to the story. I should've asked you, but maybe it's better that we waited because we're old now and . . . " He stopped to smile when she choked out a laugh. "And with all this dubious maturing I've realized something."

She sucked in a breath and lifted her worried gaze to his. "What?"

With a slight shake of his head, he bent a little and brushed his mouth over hers. "There's something I want."

"Another kiss?" she asked, her voice a hopeful whisper that made his chest both swell and ache at the same time.

"Yes," he said. "But more."

"A bunch of kisses?"

At the hint of laughter in her voice, he smiled. She'd relaxed and was teasing him. "More," he said softly.

She blinked. "You . . . want to sleep with me?"

"Oh yes," he breathed, pulling her in. "I want that, Rory. And I want it bad too. But still more."

"I . . . don't understand."

"I want something between us."

She froze. "Like . . . a condom?"

He laughed and pressed his forehead to hers. He kept thinking about what his sister said, about him giving the next woman he felt something for a shot. A real shot. He really hated to ever admit Cass might have been onto something, but he honestly had never felt this way about another woman before. "A relationship," he said and watched her mouth fall open.

"I— You—" She gulped in air. "With me?"

Now they were on the same page. A damn long time coming too. "Yes," he said and kissed her, liking the way she melted into him as if her body was way ahead of her brain at this point. "You in?"

She stared up at him. "I'm not very good at relationships," she said very seriously.

"Says who?"

This seemed to stymie her. "Every guy I've ever dated?"

"Then you've been dating the wrong guys." He rubbed his jaw to hers. "Take a chance, Rory. Take the risk."

Her hands came up to his face, her fingers slipping into his hair, and it felt so good he tightened his grip on her.

"I've got a bad track record with the people in my life," she said quietly and shook her head when he started to speak. "No, you know it's true. I'm not a good bet, Max. In fact, I'm a really bad one."

That she absolutely believed this broke his heart. She'd survived a shitty childhood and then a rough stint on her own in San Francisco. But she *had* survived, even thrived. And then there was how she'd handled tonight and all the storm had thrown at them without blinking an eye.

And yet this, with him—which should've been one of the easier things in her life—scared the hell out of her.

"You need to believe me on this," she said, backing free of him. "I'm not built that way, I'm not good at relationships. I'm not good at letting people in and keeping them. I don't know how."

He caught her and reeled her panicking body in. "It's okay," he said very gently, cupping her face, tilting it to his to make sure she heard him. "Because I do."

While she continued to stare up at him, he lowered his head and gave her a soft kiss. And then a not-so-soft kiss that he seemed to have trouble tearing himself free of. "You have no idea, do you," he murmured, "why I bring Carl in every week to get groomed. And it's not because he needs it. It's because we've both got it bad for you. We use all available opportunities as an excuse to see you."

She choked out a surprised laugh. "That is a costly way to do it."

He laughed. "I know. Do you trust me, Rory?"

"Yes," she said without a beat of hesitation.

"I wanted to drive you here," he said. "I wanted any reason at all to spend time with you. I'm serious about you, and if I'm being honest, that's been building for a long time."

He could tell by the look on her face that she was serious about him too, scared to death or not.

"I think about you," he told her.

She shook her head. "When? When do you think about me?"

"When I'm sleeping. And working. And not working." He stopped to take in her smile. "You're the one for me, Rory. And I think you feel the same way about me."

She could've lied her way out of that if she wanted. He knew she had the skills. But she didn't. Holding his gaze in hers, she backed him to the bed and then, still holding eye contact, gave him a shove to his chest that had him dropping to the mattress.

He laughed but that laughter stuck in his throat when she got on the bed and slowly climbed up his body, letting him feel her, all of her, and with a groan he began to wrap her up tight in her arms and—

That's when they were jumped by 150 pounds of dog wanting to get in on the fun, panting dog breath in their faces, making Rory laugh.

Max loved the sound and smiled at her as he reared up to kiss her, having to reach around Carl, but Rory stopped him with a hand to his chest.

He stilled. "Problem?" he asked. "Other than the heavyweight road block named Carl?"

At the sound of his name, Carl barked, excited they were finally having all the fun.

"I think maybe he's trying to tell us something," Rory said.

"Like?"

"Like . . . like maybe we're moving too fast."

"I don't think Carl's that deep of a thinker," he said. "Down."

Rory started to shift but he gripped her and with a laugh said, "Carl. *Carl*, down. You stay."

Carl promptly rolled onto his back on the bed, taking up nearly the entire thing and showing off all his bits as he did.

"Well, you did say down," Rory pointed out. "He listens. He laid down. What a good boy," she said to his dog. "Are you a good boy, Carl?"

Carl's tail thumped the bed staccato style.

Max pointed to the floor.

Carl hefted out a sigh and slunk off the mattress. Slowly. One long leg at a time, with a look back at Max as each limb hit the floor like he was hoping he'd change his mind.

Max didn't. Instead, he tucked Rory beneath him, entwined his fingers in hers, and slowly slid their hands over her head as he lowered his.

"So," he said. "Where were we?"

Chapter Nine

Rory STARED up at Max, mesmerized by the warm look in his eyes. "I think you were about to rock my world," she whispered.

He smiled. "Was I?"

Her heart sped up. God, he had a gorgeous smile. "I hope so," she said fervently.

He pulled her sweater slowly over her head. It fell to the floor and she heard him suck in a breath, which was reassuring in a sexy, "ohmigod this is happening" way because it meant she did it for him every bit as much as he did it for her.

Pressing herself up against the long, leanly muscled body she'd been dreaming about for ages, she wrapped her arms around him and pressed her face into his throat. He smelled amazing and, needing to know if he tasted amazing as well, she took a little nibble.

He growled low in his throat at that and tipped her chin up. "Tell me you're in this, Rory."

If she was any more in, she'd be drowning. "I'm in this."

He stared into her eyes for a beat as if searching for the truth in that statement, but she'd never
been so honest with anyone in her life. "I want
you, Max. I always have."

That had a fierce light blazing from his intense
eyes and then he claimed her mouth. She loved that
he wasn't gentle with her. She didn't need or want
that, and she moaned when he kissed her hard and
hot and hungry all at once. And then he was busy
divesting her of the rest of her clothing until she
was bared to him. With a shaky breath he took her
in, and when that made her shift uncomfortably,
he caught her hands and bent to press his mouth to
the throbbing pulse at the base of her neck, slowly
working his way south.

"Soft," he murmured. "So soft. Sweet too."

She managed a laugh.

He lifted his head, eyes crinkled in amusement.
"What?"

"No one's ever called me sweet before."

"Well, you do hide it well," he said demurely,
making her snort. He flicked a tongue across her
nipple and then sucked it into his mouth, leaving
her a trembling wreck. He moved south then, taking his sweet-ass time too, nipping her just beneath
her belly button, her hip. "You'll stop me if there's
anything you don't like," he said.

"At the moment, I'm more likely to beg you to
keep going."

He smiled. "Like the sound of that too." His big

hands urged her legs to part, and he lowered his head and rubbed his stubbly jaw against her inner thigh while she squirmed and wriggled.

He simply tightened his grip on her, holding her still while he turned his head and worked her other inner thigh, and then finally, finally he found a new target, the perfect spot, her holy grail spot . . . without so much as a road map or directions.

Before she could marvel over this, she was gone. Lost in wave after wave of sensation that robbed her of her senses while she burst apart at the seams.

When she surfaced back to reality, he'd located a condom from she had no idea where, but she was grateful. "Yes," she said. *"Please, yes."*

His gaze riveted on hers, his mouth curved as he kissed her. "Love the 'please,'" he murmured, voice sexy, low and rough. "Feel free to give me more of that."

She was laughing as he slid home but the laughter backed up in her throat, turning into a moan. Helplessly she arched into him, filled to bursting as he claimed her mouth again.

And then he began to move and claimed her body as well, taking her to a place she'd never been before. When they both fell apart, shuddering in each other's arms, Rory couldn't catch her breath, couldn't get it together.

She didn't have to. He held her for a long time after, rolling onto his back, taking her with him so that she was plastered all over him, a tangle of limbs. His arms remained tight around her, one hand gliding slowly up and down her back, occasionally stopping to squeeze her ass.

It made her smile and her heart sigh. She fell asleep like that, more content then she could ever remember feeling, thinking if only Christmas could end right here, it'd be perfect.

R ORY opened her eyes to find Max standing over her with a steaming cup in his hand and a sexy, knowing smile on his face.

He'd spent the past few hours rocking her world and he damn well knew it. It'd been . . . amazing, but now she was short of sleep and felt like roadkill. Probably looked like it too.

But not Max. Nope, he had the nerve to look re-energized and perfect.

With a groan, Rory rolled over and planted her face in the pillow.

"Mmm," he murmured huskily in her ear, clearly taking her new position as an invitation. "Later, if you're really, really good." And then he lightly smacked her ass. "Rise and shine, princess."

She gave him a kick but missed by a mile because he had reflexes like a cat.

He merely laughed and set the steaming cup by the bed. "A real morning person, I see."

"Anyone ever tell you that you're more fun when you're not talking?" she muttered, muffled by the pillow.

He laughed again, telling her that he *was* a morning person, which meant she might have to kill him.

"We've gotta go," he said.

With a gasp, she sat right up, clutching the sheet to her chest. "It's morning?"

"Almost. But I wanted to talk to you before we go."

Oh boy. A talk. In her experience, nothing good ever came out of a talk, and she flopped back into her facedown position.

His hand was on her ass again, squeezing now. "Of course, there're other ways to get your attention . . . "

Not before she at least brushed her teeth, there wasn't. She rolled onto her back to tell him so but he was there, right there, leaning over her, easily taking control of the sheet, tugging it southward.

"Okay, okay, I'm listening!" she claimed, tightening her tenuous grip on it.

But the sheet still slid south, with Max watching from warm, sexy, hooded eyes as she was revealed to him inch by inch until the sheet rested just below her hips.

Leaving her bare-ass naked on the bed.

With a squeak, she reached for the covers, but with a grin, he held them out of her reach, heavy sexual intent in his gaze.

Carl, mistaking the commotion as fun time, jumped up with a bark.

"Sorry, buddy," Max said. "She's all mine."

The words should've annoyed the hell out of Rory; instead they gave her a hot rush. *All his . . .*

Nudging the dog aside and dropping the sheet onto the floor, Max snatched Rory and pulled her in.

He was dressed. He smelled fresh and clean and his hair was wet.

The day had started without her.

"I don't do talks while naked," she managed, once again trying to reach for the covers.

Max leaned in a little further, taking hold of her wrists, sliding them up the bed, alongside of her head. "Let me offer an incentive." He kissed her, starting with the lightest brush of lips against hers but working up both the pressure and the heat. When he finally pulled back, she wasn't the only one trying to catch her breath. She'd forgotten her rush, and the fact that she hadn't brushed her teeth; she forgot *everything* but him and had turned her wrists so that her hands clasped his hard enough for her nails to leave marks on him.

Straightening, he took a slow, deep breath and let it out, making her realize with some shock and a lot of female pride that he was just as affected as she. "I just wanted to make sure you understand my intentions," he said. "And what I want."

She snorted and rocked against a most impressive erection. "I think I know what you want."

He didn't smile. Not even a twitch of his lips. Instead, his eyes filled with something she couldn't quite catch.

"What I want," he said, "is significantly more

than a road trip from hell and a quick relief of some fairly serious sexual tension."

She stared at him. "You mean the relationship you mentioned last night."

"Yes."

"For how long?"

His gaze never left hers. "Until we don't want each other anymore."

She couldn't even imagine not wanting him, and his lips twitched like he could read her mind. Leaning in again, he pressed his mouth to the spot between her breasts.

Over her heart.

"I'm feeling a little self-conscious," she whispered.

"Funny, that's not what I'm feeling."

No kidding. She could feel him hard as stone through his jeans. "I need caffeine," she whispered.

"Here." He handed her the cup.

She sipped, aware of the way his eyes heated every inch of her body as they roamed over her.

Seemed only fair since just the thought of him naked made breathing difficult.

"Better?" he asked.

She managed a nod.

That made him smile. "You're cute in the mornings," he said. "If we had more time, I'd show you just how sexy I find that, but it's time to rise and shine. The roads are open and it's only six o'clock."

"We can get all the way through to Tahoe?"

He smiled. "Merry Christmas, Rory."

Chapter Ten

Rory speed showered and pulled on clothes, and they were out the door not ten minutes later.

"Breakfast?" Max asked, pointing to the small continental spread in the check-in area.

"No," she said. "I'm sorry, I just need to get there."

He didn't say anything until he had them loaded and on the highway. "Need to get there?" he repeated curiously. "Yesterday it was 'want to get there.'"

Yes, and she was extremely aware of the difference. She just didn't want to explain it, how she felt she'd managed to fail her family yet again. She pulled out her phone to call her mom but she still didn't have reception. The curse of the Sierra Mountains.

Max's hand settled on her thigh and then Carl's head came over the seat and settled on her shoulder. Rory's heart warmed from the inside out and she heard herself start talking. "When I told my stepdad I was coming, he had me pick up my mom's present from him. It's a necklace he had special ordered and made in the city. It was supposed to be ready a few days ago but got held up. I told him I'd hand deliver it. He was understandably hesitant to believe me since I haven't been home in so long, but I promised." She paused. "But they always open presents by dawn. I obviously screwed it all up."

"Hold on," Max said. "The present was going to be late anyway, but you offered to pick it up and hand deliver it. You set a deadline on yourself, and now because you missed that you think you failed them? Do I have that right?"

"You don't understand," she said. "I've made promises to come home before and haven't come through. I wanted this to be different."

"It *is* different. You're actually going. And if not for the storm and then my truck and Carl, you'd have been there."

"Not your fault," she said, reaching out to put her hand on his arm. "All those things were out of your control."

He slid her a quick look, his eyes warm. "Yeah, and remember that, Rory. Remember the very same thing. None of this is your fault."

An hour and a half later they made it up and over the summit and into their small Tahoe town. It was just barely eight o'clock. Definitely past her self-imposed deadline, but still early. Hopefully early enough, but her heart was pounding with anxiety.

Max pulled into the driveway of her childhood home. The place was a small ranch-style house, emphasis on *small*, in a neighborhood of hard-working people who didn't spare a lot of time or money on their yards. Not that it mattered because the new snowfall was a white blanket over everything as far as the eye could see, giving new life to the tired street, making it indeed look like Christmas.

"Rory," Max said quietly, once again putting a hand on her thigh. "Breathe."

Right. She'd been holding her breath. She gulped in some air but she was close to a nervous breakdown. Hands sweating, she made herself busy gathering her stuff because a good part of her nerves, she suddenly realized, was from the thought of saying goodbye to Max.

He'd made his interest in her clear but she still felt a moment of panic that she'd somehow misunderstood. "Thanks for the ride," she said quickly as she slid out of the truck, grabbing her bag. "I appreciate—"

Max got out of the truck as well, and then was there, right there at her side, pulling her around to face him. "I'll drive you back to the city whenever you're ready to go."

"I can take the bus—"

"I'll drive you," he said firmly.

"But I don't want to cut your visit with your family short—"

"I'm taking you back," he said right over her. Calm. Sure. Absolutely adamant. "Whatever day and time you want. I'll call you in a little bit to see how you're doing, and you can call me too. Any time." He bent a little to look right into her eyes. "Repeat after me, Rory. Any time."

She stared into his dark green eyes and felt something catch in her heart. Or maybe it was just rolling over and exposing its tender underbelly. "Any time," she whispered.

"Because this isn't over," he said and waited for her to repeat that as well.

"Max—"

"You wanted to give me a Christmas present," he said quietly. "This is it. This is what I want."

"Me?"

"*You.*"

Warmth filled her, and not just her good spots. She felt cherished, wanted, cared for . . . and she felt something else—a huge smile on her face. She couldn't control it. "And I didn't even have to wrap it."

He relaxed and smiled back, and then leaned in for a kiss just as Carl stuck his big head out the truck's still open door and licked Rory from chin to forehead.

She laughed while Max cupped the dog's face in his big palm and pushed him back into the truck. He turned to Rory then, his smile fading as he looked past her to the front door. She followed his gaze and froze at the sight of her stepdad standing on the porch, arms crossed, face creased in the stern frown that had framed her entire youth.

"You're here," he called out. "Thought maybe you'd changed your mind."

Again. He didn't say the word but she felt it shimmering in the air between them. "I didn't." The warm fuzzies of a moment ago were fading fast, leaving her chilled, more than the snow around her. "I'm sorry I'm late, but—"

"No one expected you to get here on any sort of timetable."

Okay, she got it, she was the screw-up once again, but damn. It hurt more than she thought to be on the other side and be judged for who she'd once been. "You don't understand, this time was different—"

"Actually, I do understand and I'm not surprised—"

"Hold on," Max said and grabbed Rory's hand. "You haven't let her talk."

Her stepdad looked at him. "Max Stranton. What are you doing here?"

"I'm Rory's boyfriend," he said so easily that Rory's heart skipped a beat. "The storm slowed us down," Max went on. "The roads were a mess."

"You two okay?" her stepdad asked.

"Yes," Max said. "But we stopped to help an older couple with a flat, and then my dog took off on us. Rory could've gotten a ride from the one car who'd stopped but she stayed to help me find Carl."

Her stepdad looked at Rory.

"I'm sorry if I've disappointed you," she said, "but there was no way I could just take the ride and leave Max alone on the summit in the storm with his dog missing."

"Of course not," her stepdad said.

Rory blinked. Was that . . . understanding in her stepdad's voice? Still stunned at that, she turned to Max when he said her name. He cupped the nape of her neck in a big palm and pulled her in for a quick but warm kiss. "Any time," he said softly. "Yeah?"

"Yeah."

"Even if it's in a few hours."

She let out a half laugh that was more like a sob so she cut it off. "I already told you, I won't cut your visit short—"

"Or yours," her stepdad said. He'd left the front porch and had come closer. "Your mom and sisters are going to be thrilled you made it, Rory."

She looked at him. "Really?"

He gestured with his chin and turned to the front door, where her mom and her three half sisters waited with welcoming smiles on their faces, waving. They were all still in their PJ's, keeping them inside, but at their clear joy at seeing her she felt a lump in her throat.

"It's Christmas," her stepdad said quietly. "And you're actually here. Merry Christmas, Rory. Welcome home. We'll wait inside for you." And then with one look at Max standing strong and tall at her side, he turned and headed back to the house.

Max pulled her into him. "Knew you could handle this."

"How?" she asked in marvel. "I mean, I've been with me for twenty-three years and I still don't get me."

He let out a low laugh and pressed his forehead

to hers. "I was a little slow on the uptake, but I've got you now and I don't plan for that to change."

Her breath caught. That sounded a whole lot like her greatest fantasy come true.

"There's one more thing." He nudged her face up. "I love you, Rory. I think I always have."

Emotion flooded her and her knees wobbled. "I need to sit."

Max urged her back a few steps to his still open truck. When she was once again in the passenger seat, he crouched in front of her. "Still with me?"

Her heart had started to pound. She'd never thought to hear the L-word from anyone, much less him, but there it was, out in the open. She should have known it would be like that with him. Honest. Straightforward. She looked into his eyes and nodded. "Still here."

"Did you just nearly pass out when I told you my feelings?" he asked.

"No. I nearly passed out when I realized something."

"What?"

"That I think feel the same way," she whispered like this was a state secret, loving the way it made him smile all the way to his eyes, allowing her to access a well of courage she hadn't known she'd had. She slid her fingers into his hair, which she now knew would make him purr like a cat, a big, wild cat. "I love you, Max." She paused and then let out a small smile as she repeated his vow. "I think I always have."

His low laugh warmed her to the far corners of her heart and he pulled her in for a tight squeeze. "I'll be back for you. You going to be okay?"

She realized she'd been holding her breath again, for what she had no idea. For him to change his mind? Laugh? Take it all back? "So . . . that's it?" she asked. "You love me, I love you, the end?"

"For now," he said.

"And later?"

He lifted a shoulder. "We can talk about our next step."

"Which would be . . . ?" she asked.

He kissed the tension away and then pulled back far enough to say, "Whatever you want."

"What about what you want?" she asked, breathless. She was pretty sure he kissed her just to leave her in a state.

He stroked the hair from her face. "I want it all."

Oh. Well, that sounded . . . promising. And exciting. She was so happy she yanked him in and kissed him until both of them were breathless. "Merry Christmas," she whispered against his lips. "I'll give you your *real* present later."

He smiled sexily. "Sounds promising."

She smiled back. "It is."

HOLIDAY WISHES

Chapter One

To say Sean felt stressed was a huge understatement. Give him a cliff to scale or a bar brawl to break up. Hell, give him a freight train to try to outrun, *anything* but having to pull off being the best man for his brother Finn's wedding—including but not limited to keeping said brother from losing his collective shit.

It's not like Sean didn't understand. Getting married was a big deal. Okay, so he didn't fully understand, not really, but he wanted to. He really did. And how funny was that? Sean O'Riley, younger brother, hook-up king extraordinaire, was suddenly tired of the game and found himself aching for his own forever after.

"We almost there?" Finn asked him from the backseat of the vehicle Sean was driving.

"Yep."

"And you double checked on our reservations?"

"Yep."

"No, I'm serious, man," Finn said. "Remember when you took me to Vegas and when we got there, every hotel was booked and we had to stay at the Magic-O motel?"

"Man, a guy screws up one time . . ."

"We had a stripper pole in our rooms, Sean."

Sean sighed. "Okay, but to be fair, that was back when I was still in my stupid phase. I promise you that we have reservations—no stripper poles. I even double and triple checked, just like you asked me a hundred and one times. Pru, I hope you real- ize you're marrying a nag."

Pru, Finn's fiancée, laughed from the shotgun position. "Hey, one of us has to be the nag in this relationship, and it isn't me."

Sean held up a palm and Pru leaned over the console to give him a high-five.

"Just so you know," Sean said to Finn, "I didn't pick this place, your woman did."

"True story," Pru said. "The B&B's closed to the public this entire weekend. Sean booked the whole place for our bachelor/bachelorette party weekend extravaganza."

"I superheroed this thing," Sean said.

Finn snorted and let loose of a small smile because they both knew that for most of Sean's childhood, that's what he'd aspired to be, a superhero—sans tights though. Tights had never been Sean's thing, especially after suffering through them for two seasons in high school football before he'd merci- fully cracked his clavicle.

After that, he'd turned to fighting, and not the good kind either. Finn, physically older by seven years, mentally older by about a hundred, had single-handedly saved Sean from just about every situation he'd ever landed himself in. Thanks to Finn, there'd been a lot fewer situations than there should've been and it hadn't been for lack of trying.

Fact was, everyone knew Sean had taken the slowest possible route on his way to growing up, complete with plenty of detours, but he'd hit his stride now. Or at least he hoped so because Finn was counting on him in a big way over the next week and Sean had let him down enough for a lifetime. He wouldn't let him down now.

Sean pulled into the B&B's parking lot and turned to face the crowd he'd driven from San Francisco to Napa. And he did mean crowd. They'd had to rent a fourteen-seat passenger van to fit everyone, and he was the weekend's designated driver.

Oh, how times had changed. "Ready?" he asked.

Finn nodded. Pru was bouncing up and down in her seat with excitement. Willa, her BFF, was doing the same. Keane, Willa's boyfriend, opened the door for everyone to tumble out.

It was two weeks before Christmas and the rolling hills of Napa Valley were lined with grape vines for as far as the eye could see, not that they could actually see them right now. It was late, pitch dark, and rain had been pouring down steadily all day, which didn't detract from the beauty of the Victorian B&B in front of them. It did, however, detract from Sean's eagerness to go out in the rain to get to it though.

Not Pru and Willa. The two raced through the downpour laughing and holding hands with Elle, Colbie, Kylie, and Tina—the rest of Pru's posse—moving more cautiously in deference to the preservation of their heels. Sean, Finn, and Finn's posse—Archer, Keane, Spence, and Joe—followed.

They all tumbled in the front door of the B&B and stopped short in awe of the place decorated with what had to be miles of garland and lights, along with a huge Christmas tree done up in all the bells and whistles. This place could've passed for Santa's own house.

Collectively the group "oohed" and "aahed" before turning expectedly to Sean.

This was because he was actually in charge of the weekend's activities that would lead up to the final countdown to the wedding happening next week at a winery about twenty minutes up the road. This was what a best man did apparently, take care of stuff. *All* the stuff. And that Finn had asked Sean to be his best man in the first place over any of the close friends with them this weekend had the pride overcoming his anxiety of screwing it all up.

But the anxiety was making a real strong bid right at the moment. He shook off some of the raindrops and started to head over to the greeting desk and eleven people began to follow. He stopped and was nearly plowed over by the parade. "Wait here," he instructed, pausing until his very excited group nodded in unison.

Jesus. He shouldn't have poured them that champagne to pre-game before they'd left O'Riley's, the pub he and Finn owned and operated in San Francisco. And that he was the voice of reason right now was truly the irony of the century. "Stay," he said firmly and then made his way past the towering Christmas tree lit to within an inch of its life, past the raging fire in the fireplace with candles lining the mantel . . . to the small, quaint check-in desk that had a plate with some amazing looking cookies and a sign that said: YES, THESE ARE FOR YOU—WELCOME!

"Yum," Pru said and took one for each hand.

She hadn't "stayed." And neither had Finn. They both flanked Sean, munching on the cookies.

A woman sat at the check-in desk with a laptop, her fingers a blur, the tip of her Santa hat quivering as she typed away. She looked up and smiled as she took in the group. That is until her gaze landed on Sean and she froze.

He'd already done the same because holy shit—

"Greetings," she said, recovering first and so quickly that no one else seemed to notice as she stood and smiled warmly at everyone *but* Sean. "Welcome to the Hartford B&B. My name's Charlotte Hartford and I'm the innkeeper here. How can I help you?"

Good question. And Sean had the answer on the tip of his tongue, which was currently stuck to the roof of his mouth because he hadn't been prepared for this sweet and sassy redheaded blast from his past.

It'd been what, nearly a decade? He didn't know exactly because his brain wasn't functioning at full capacity, much less capable of simple math at the moment. The last time he'd seen Lotti, they'd been sixteen-year-old kids and at a high school football game. It'd been back in those dark, dark times after he and Finn had lost their parents and Sean had been at his most wild. Still, he'd somehow managed to sweet-talk the kindest, most gentle girl in school out of her virginity, losing his own in the process.

Finn nudged Sean, prompting him to clear his throat and speak. "We're here to check in. We're the Finn O'Riley party." He smiled. "It's really great to see you, Lotti. How're things?"

She cocked her head to the side and looked out the window. "Well the storm's certainly been challenging. I heard the roads were bad, so wasn't sure you'd all even be able to get here. I'm glad you made it. So, the O'Ryan party . . ." She turned to her computer. "I'll get you checked in."

"O'Riley," Sean corrected. And why was she playing like she didn't know him? "Lotti, it's me. Sean."

"O'Riley," she repeated, fingers clicking the keyboard. "Yes, here you all are. Twelve guests, two nights. Wine tasting tour tomorrow. Bachelor/bachelorette here tomorrow night. Checking out Sunday morning." She then proceeded to check them in with quick efficiency, managing to avoid Sean's direct gaze the entire time.

It wasn't until she handed him a room key and their fingers touched that she actually met his gaze, her own warm chocolate one clear and startled.

Again she recovered quickly, lifting her chin and turning away.

"You really going to pretend you don't remember me?" he asked quietly.

She didn't answer. This, of course, delighted Finn to no end. He grinned wide at Sean as they all turned to head up the stairs to their rooms.

"What's so funny?" Sean snapped.

"It finally happened. You being put in your place by a woman. And she was hot too."

Pru cuffed Finn upside the back of his head.

"I mean she was smart and funny and had a great personality," Finn said.

Pru rolled her eyes.

"And," Finn went on, "she didn't remember you. That's the best part. Where do you know her from anyway?"

Sean shook his head. "Never mind."

The ass that called himself Sean's brother was still chortling to himself when they all vanished into their respective rooms. Because the B&B had only six guest rooms total, and eight of their group were coupled off, the four singles had been forced to pair up. Sean keyed himself into the room he was going to share with Joe. They both tossed their duffel bags onto each of the two beds.

Twin beds. And shit, those beds were *small*.

Sean stood there hands on hips. The bedding

was thick and comfortable looking, but done up in a girlie floral print and situated *way* too close to Joe's bed to please him.

Joe was looking less than pleased himself. "Damn."

"Yeah. Sucks to be single in a wedding party."

"Yeah," Joe agreed. "But hey, positive spin—it doesn't suck to be single." He flopped onto his bed and grabbed the remote, bringing up an MMA fight.

Sean blew out a breath and turned to the door.

"It's nearly midnight," Joe said to his back. "Where you off to? Back down to the hot chick who didn't recognize you?"

"She totally recognized me," Sean said.

"Right."

"She did."

"Dude, then that's even worse."

Sean flipped him off and left as Joe laughed, heading back down the stairs. Because Joe was right, being recognized and ignored *was* worse. And it was all his own fault.

The night had gotten noisy. Wind battered the old Victorian, rattling the windows, causing the trees outside to brush against the walls, which creaked and groaned under the strain. Sean hoped like hell that the carpenters back in the day had known what they were doing and that the place would hold.

For the second time in ten minutes, he strode up to the check-in desk. Pru had been the one to insist on this B&B because it'd been built in the late 1800s and had a cool history that he'd been told about in great detail but couldn't repeat to save his life because he hadn't listened. All he knew was that Pru had wanted to stay here so badly that he'd made it happen for her.

But it didn't mean he had to like it.

Lotti was no longer in sight. There was a small bell for service on the desk and just as he reached out to hit it, he heard a male voice from inside what looked to be an office.

"I'm sorry, Charlotte," the unseen man was saying. "But you know we're not working. You're so closed off that I can't get close to you."

Sean froze for two reasons. One, Lotti had always hated her full name. Hated it to the bone so much she'd refused to answer to it.

And two . . . those words. *You're so closed off that I can't get close to you . . .* They reverberated in Sean's head, pulling memories he'd shoved deep. That long-ago summer night they'd shared had been the accumulation of several years of platonic friendship, started when he'd needed help in English and she in chemistry. They'd tutored each other, the perennial bad boy and the perennial good girl, and then one night they'd been each other's world in the back of her dad's pickup on the bluffs of Marin Headlands.

Afterward, she'd told him she loved him. He could remember staring into her sweet eyes and nearly swallowing his own tongue. *Love?* Was that what this all-consuming, heart and gut wrenching emotion he felt for her was? And even though he'd suspected that yes indeed it'd been love, he'd wanted no part of it because it hurt like hell.

And then proving just that, she'd gone on to tell him that her family was moving away, but since they were in love, they could stay in touch and write and call and visit.

She was going to leave. Even with all he'd felt for her, he'd known he wouldn't, couldn't, be the guy she'd needed. She'd indeed written him, and being the chicken-shit, emotionally stunted kid he'd been back then, he hadn't written back. Or returned her calls. Losing her had been like a red-hot poker to the chest but he hadn't been able to see himself in a long-distance relationship, or in any relationship at all.

Hell, he couldn't have committed to a dentist appointment back then.

He'd thought of her, always with a smile and an ache in his chest because he deeply regretted how he'd behaved. By the time he graduated, he'd grown up enough to try to find her to apologize, but he'd had no luck. He'd never seen her again—until now.

A guy came out of the office, presumably the one who'd spoken, and headed straight for the front door, walking out into the storm without looking back.

Sean waited a minute, but there was only silence coming from the office. No sign of Lotti, nor a single sound. Clearly it was the worst possible time to try to talk to her, but her eerie silence worried him.

Then suddenly came the sound of glass shattering, but before he could rush into the room, she came out.

She wasn't crying, which was a huge relief. Her eyes were . . . blank, actually, giving nothing away. That is until she saw Sean. Then they sparked, but not the good kind of spark.

"You," she said.

Yep, he had the bad timing thing down pat.

Chapter Two

OF COURSE Sean O'Riley would be the one standing there, witness to the fact that she had a problem letting people in. Gee, wonder where she'd learned such a thing.

Unfortunately, she couldn't turn back time. He'd clearly overheard her being dumped by Trevor, a guy she'd gone out with six and a half times. The half date had been the other night when he'd brought her dinner and had pushed the issue of becoming lovers.

She hadn't been ready and he'd been frustrated with her. She got that, she did, but intimacy was a big—and not easy—step for her and dammit, she'd just needed a little more time. Trevor had said he understood, but clearly that hadn't been true. He'd dumped her.

In earshot of her first lover.

Perfect.

And that *that* was her only concern at the moment told her everything she needed to know about her real feelings for Trevor. Clearly, it would never have worked out. Not that this eased her embarrassment one little bit. Honestly, she couldn't see how this night could get any worse and with a sigh, she met Sean's gaze.

And holy cow, an age-old tingle of awareness and heat sliced through her. She decided to attribute this to the fact that he was still sex-on-a-stick, maybe even more so now. Back then he'd been trouble with a capital *T*, but with such charisma that he'd been like the Pied Piper. She'd followed him right to her own undoing.

And she had a feeling not much had changed.

"Is there a problem with your room?" she asked politely, hoping to get rid of him quickly.

But she should've known better. Sean smiled that smile that had once had her panties melting right off. "Yeah," he said. "The bed's too small." He was taller than she remembered and leanly muscled. His hair was still dark but with some lighter streaks from the sun and messily tousled, most likely courtesy of his own restless fingers. His eyes still shined with more mischievousness than any one man should hold.

Not going there, she told herself just as a gust of wind knocked the house like a bolt of lightning. The lights flickered as the electricity surged and she held her breath. This old building could barely tolerate the electrical needs in decades past, so the demands they put on it in the here and now were always a gamble. Luckily the guests they had always seemed charmed if the electricity went out, and she made sure to keep lots of candles and lanterns around. Plus, she had a generator if she needed. But tonight she didn't want any problems. Not when her biggest problem was standing in front of her looking good enough to eat, damn him.

Another gust of wind hit hard and the electricity blinked on and off again. *Please don't go out, please don't go out . . .*

It went out.

"Are you serious with tonight?" she asked karma or fate, or whoever was in charge of such things.

She heard a rough laugh and then Sean accessed the flashlight on his phone. "This is your fault," she said.

His brows went up and she sighed. "Don't ask me how, it just is. It has to be."

She could see him smiling through the glow. It was that patented bad boy smile and in spite of herself, her heart gave a treacherous little sigh. She hardened both it and her voice. "Thank you," she said with as much dignity as she could muster, leaning on her desk in order to keep her hands off the guy who still had a solo starring role in her every sexual fantasy, and had since high school. A fact she'd take to the grave, thank you very much. And okay, not *every* single fantasy—the Chrises had occasional starring roles as well; Chris Hemsworth, Chris Pine, Chris Pratt . . .

With a sigh, she turned to her desk, a hundred-year-old hand-carved piece, the top inlaid with time-worn leather, the edges rough with life's battle marks. It'd been her father's, a man who'd never wavered in his love for her mom, not once in the thirty years they'd had before he died last year. And yet he'd died of cancer that he hadn't told a soul about, not her mom, not Lotti, no one, nor had he had it treated.

Because that thought led to a dark tunnel that she hadn't yet found a light for, she shook it off and pulled open a desk drawer to grab a Maglite and a box of matches. She'd already had a bunch of candles lit on the mantel so they weren't in the complete dark, but she needed to check on everyone. "I'm sorry, but I don't have a different room to switch you to," she said to Sean. "If you'll excuse me, I need to go check on the other guests."

"It's late," he said. "Everyone's in their rooms. Trust me, they'd come out if they needed something from you."

She cocked her head to listen, but not a soul was moving.

"Not even a mouse," he said with a smile, reading her mind. Then he took her Maglite and beamed it up the stairs. "See? No one. They're all in bed. Tell me what else you need to do, I'll help."

"Hmm," she said.

"And that means . . . ?"

"The last time you '*helped*' me, it'd been to remove my jeans," she said, then bit her traitorous tongue. Where had that come from? Oh yeah, it'd come from her very, *very* stupid side.

He winced, like the memories of their past hurt him as much as they did her. Whatever. She wasn't going to be drawn in. She'd lost more than just her virginity that night. She'd lost a chunk of her heart. Not that she wanted it back . . .

Grabbing her flashlight back, she headed for the stairs. "I want to walk the hallway just in case someone needs something." When he followed her, she gave him a long look. "I can handle this."

"Humor me," he said.

So they walked the hallway together, didn't hear a peep out of anyone, and went back downstairs. Because the house was so old, she moved to the front door. She needed to go outside to check the electric panel to see if she'd blown any fuses. She pulled on her jacket and was surprised when she opened the door to find Sean once again coming with her.

He pulled up her hood for her, tucking her hair in, which felt oddly . . . intimate. "You don't have to do this," she yelled. She had to. The wind and rain had whipped up the night so that she could hardly hear her own voice.

"You blame me for this mess. The least I can do is see it through with you."

They ran along the path and around to the side of the house, all while being pelted by the storm. Under the roof's overhang, Lotti stopped, panting for breath. "Here," she said, handing him the flashlight to hold for her so she could pry open the electrical panel. "And I don't really blame you for tonight," she admitted grudgingly to the panel, not wanting to let him off the hook entirely.

Sean moved in closer so that his front brushed

her back, protecting her from the worst of the storm with his body. "But you blame me for hurting you, as you should. Trust me, I blame me too. I wish that I'd done things differently."

She closed her eyes against the onslaught of emotions that battered her at his close proximity. "No," she said. "It's not all on you. I wanted you that night. But I do blame you for turning me into a serial monogamist."

He turned her to face him. He'd made sure to pull up her hood, but he didn't have one. His dark hair was drenched and looked midnight black, his way-too-handsome face a perfect backdrop for those startlingly sharp green eyes. "Explain."

"No."

"Try again."

She tossed up her hands. "Fine. You were my first one-night stand and it didn't work out, okay? I mean not even a little! First, it wasn't all that great and second, I thought we were going to be a couple, which you clearly *never* intended. Because of you, I learned to be cautious and careful and became a—"

"—serial monogamist," he repeated, eyes narrowed. "I get it. But back up a second. It wasn't . . . 'all that great'?"

Okay, so she'd totally lied there. She'd thought it might put a halt to this awkward conversation. "This conversation is going to have to get in line behind my other more pressing problems."

"'Wasn't all that great,'" he was echoing to himself. "Yeah, I'm going to need you to explain that."

Oh boy. She wracked her brain for a legitimate gripe. "Well it was over pretty fast and—" She broke off when his eyebrows shot up so far they vanished into his hair.

"It was over pretty fast?" he repeated, so obviously stunned at this tidbit that she had to laugh.

"You're starting to sound like a parrot," she said.

"Just coming to terms with what an asshole I was back then. But in my defense, I was sixteen and pretty stupid."

And grieving. She had to give him that. He'd lost both of his parents in a tragic car accident. At the time, she couldn't imagine the pain he'd been suffering. All she'd wanted to do was take his mind off things.

She was pretty sure she'd done that, at least for a few hours. First, they'd shared some pilfered alcohol, and then he'd kissed her. And oh how good *that* had felt. Until that night, she'd never gone further than a kiss before. Everything Sean had done had turned her on. *Everything*. Until he'd tried to slow her down.

But the alcohol had been like liquid courage and she'd been on the very edge of her first social orgasm. Slowing down hadn't been an option for her and she'd pushed for more. She'd gotten her wish and he'd been sweet and gentle. He'd gone slow, so achingly slow that in the end, she'd been begging him. But they'd been drinking and he hadn't wanted to go all the way. He'd been worried and concerned for her, but she'd pushed the issue, taking the lead, taking him into her body. He'd been buried deep and trembling with the effort to hold back for her when from the front of her dad's truck she'd heard her cell phone going off.

She'd been way past curfew.

It'd been the call to bring her out, to dash her with the proverbial bucket of ice water. The fear of her parents finding out what she'd been up to with "the horrible, rotten, no-good O'Riley boy," and she'd lost her mojo.

Not exactly his fault . . .

"I love you," she'd whispered and she'd never forget the look of panic on his face. She should've suspected it then, but it'd still been such a shock when after she'd moved out of the city he hadn't followed through with his promise about seeing her, not once. With all her ridiculously young heart she'd wanted forever with him. She'd called, written him letters, and she'd poured her heart out in each and every one. He'd never responded and she'd never seen him again.

In hindsight, she knew they'd been far too young for anything serious. They'd both needed more life experiences and maturity. Not that her heart appreciated the reasoning.

"I can promise you," he said, "I've learned a whole lot since then."

The words made certain parts of her anatomy quiver, which she ignored. "Whatever you say." She turned from him and eyeballed the electrical panel. Just as she thought, she'd blown a fuse. She pulled it out and replaced it with one of the spares she had tucked into the panel for just such incidents.

The electricity came back on.

"Impressive," Sean said.

"What, that a woman might know how to work an electrical panel for her hundred-plus-year-old house?"

"No," he said. "I know how smart you are. I meant it's impressive the lengths you'll go to in order to avoid a real conversation with me."

She blew out a breath. "There's nothing left to talk about."

"I disagree. There's the matter of the 'not that good' thing."

"Oh for God's sake!" She turned to face him. "I take it back, all right? I'll put an ad on Craigslist and shout it from the rooftops. Would that make you feel better?"

"No. But getting a chance to make it up to you would."

"In bed, I'm guessing."

"Preferably. But a bed isn't required."

She stared at him and then had to laugh at his audacity. That was all she needed, to get too close and fall for him again. "Pass, but thanks for the offer."

"See," he said. "You *did* mean it."

"Look, I'm sorry if you're insulted by my memory of our one night. But I'm not interested in revisiting it or in having this conversation." She moved around him and dashed back toward the B&B.

With him right behind her.

They stood inside the foyer and did their best to shake off from the rain. Unfortunately, the foyer was small. Too small, and sharing it with him made it seem to shrink even more. She inadvertently brushed against him removing her jacket and another bolt of awareness zinged her.

Back in high school, Sean had been lanky lean, almost to the point of being too skinny. But he'd filled in since then, big time. There was nothing boy-like about him anymore. The Sean she'd known was now *all* man.

Tearing her gaze off of him, she hung up her jacket and couldn't help herself. She dropped her forehead to the wall and banged it a few times. It'd been a long day, and a longer night.

Sean put a hand on her shoulder. "Hey," he said softly. "You okay?"

No, dammit. She wasn't. She lifted her head. "Fine."

"I'm sorry about that ass-munch who dumped you."

She found a laugh. "How do you know he was an ass-munch?"

"Because he called you Charlotte."

She let out another low, rough laugh. Better than tears. "Yes," she said. "Because that's my name."

"You hate being called Charlotte."

"That's what I go by these days."

He held her gaze captive. "Why?"

She shrugged. "It's more professional, I guess.

It's a woman's name, not a girl's." She inhaled deeply and managed to keep the eye contact, no easy thing to do. He could charm secrets out of a nun. "No one's called me Lotti in a very long time."

He surprised her by taking a step toward her, closing the already small distance. "I'm sorry if you're hurting," he murmured with a surprising amount of compassion in his voice.

"I'm not." She paused and let out a breath. "At all, actually. Which is the problem."

His gaze never left hers. "I'm still sorry. For a lot of things."

The Sean of old had been a lot of things; wild to the point of being practically feral, as rough and tumble as they came, and *way* too smart for his own good. Deep in his own head because of his grief, what he *hadn't* been was particularly aware of anyone's pain but his own. "Who are you and what have you done with Sean O'Riley?" she asked.

He shrugged. "Maybe you're not the only one who grew up."

She knew that very well could be true, but the odds were against him. And she told herself she didn't care. She had two days left of work and then she was off for two weeks. Two entire weeks! It'd been forever since she'd had any sort of vacation. As in literally forever. She'd gone right from high school to business school, and from business school to running the B&B for her family.

Her mom had happily retired to hand her over

the reins and was on a cruise with her sister for the holidays. Lotti didn't have any siblings, though she was as close to her cousin Garrett as she would be a brother. But he wasn't around this Christmas. No one in her family was, so she and her mom had agreed to close the B&B for the next two weeks, allowing Lotti some desperately needed time off. It wasn't a coincidence that she'd picked this time of year. Last Christmas had been a traumatic nightmare what with her dad's passing right before and then getting un-engaged right after.

Lotti didn't just want to get out of town for the holiday, she desperately *needed* to go.

"It's a nice place here," Sean said, looking around. "It suits you, running a B&B."

Why *that* made her want to glow with pleasure, she had no idea. "Thanks. I love it on most days."

His smile was wry, letting her know that he understood today *wasn't* one of those love-it days. Which made her feel a little bit like a jerk. "So what do you do for work?" she asked, genuinely wanting to know more about him. Which was so not good.

He looked a little surprised at the question, which made her feel even worse. "Finn and I own a pub in the city. O'Riley's."

She had to smile. "Talk about a job suiting a person. That sounds perfect for you."

Their gazes met and held and warmth went through her, specifically her good spots, which sent off inner warnings. *Danger, danger . . .* "It's

getting pretty late," she said. "I should lock up for
the night and go to bed. I'll see you all tomorrow
morning for breakfast and then again for the party
tomorrow night, as I'll be your server. Then once
more Sunday morning when you check out."

He gave her a small smile. "You don't have to
look so happy about that last part. Do you have
Christmas plans, is that it?"

Sure. That sounded much more logical than the
fact that she needed to get far, far away from home
and the memories here. "I do."

"Did you make a list and check it twice?"

She had to smile at that. She'd always been extremely organized and a list maker. That he remembered such a thing surprised her. "Yes, I did
as a matter of fact. I asked for kittens and rainbows
and peace on earth."

"A cynic," he said on a smile. "I didn't see that
coming."

She started to laugh but caught herself. "Listen. I don't want you to take this personally," she
said. "But I've had a rough year. I've screwed up
some pretty big things, I've worked too hard, and
I'm tired. But life is short. Too short. I'm going to
learn to eat some of the cookies I bake instead of
giving them all away to guests. I'm going to read
sappy books with happy-ever-after endings instead of book club reads that make me want to kill
myself. I'm going to sing in the rain and jump in
the puddles no matter what shoes I'm wearing. In
fact, I'm going to do it barefoot without worrying

about getting a gangrene infection from a cut. I'm going to live life to the fullest, Sean. No regrets."

He studied her for a moment and nodded. "I'm all for that."

"Glad you approve. I'm going on a two-week vacation when you all leave," she said. "I'm going to Cabo. And you can trust me when I say that I've never needed anything more than this trip because . . ." She broke off both speaking and eye contact for a beat, realizing she was revealing far too much. "Well it's a long story."

He looked at her for a moment and she thought maybe he was about to say something, but he seemed to change his mind, instead giving her another small smile.

"I hope it's everything you want it to be," he said and she could tell he meant it.

She nodded and gave him a far more genuine smile than she had before. "Thanks."

TWENTY minutes later, Lotti lay on her bed in her nine hundred square foot studio apartment above the garage and storage building. Her dad had renovated it for her when she'd come home from college and she loved it. It gave her separation from the B&B, privacy, and yet was a huge convenience if a guest needed anything after hours.

She didn't have much in it; a love seat, her bed, a small kitchen table, and her inheritance from her dad—Peaches the parrot.

"You're late!" Peaches yelled.

She'd forgotten to cover him up for sleep time. She got out of bed and draped a towel over his cage. "Goodnight, Peaches."

"I can still see you!"

Even after nearly a year together, Lotti and Peaches weren't quite yet friends. "Quiet time," she said.

"The meat loaf's dry," Peaches yelled. "You ruined my meat loaf!"

Lotti's dad had thought it was funny to teach Peaches to be a nagging housewife. "Go to sleep."

Peaches sighed and didn't utter another word.

Lotti got back into bed. Her toes and fingers were frozen to the bone as she huddled under the covers warming herself up with thoughts of sandy beaches and endless sun.

She slept deeply and the next day she worked on the accounting books while her guests took a wine tasting tour with Sean as their DD. That had interested her because the Sean of old hadn't been a guy to stand back and let others have all the fun.

But they'd come back with everyone but Sean feeling no pain and she'd had to admit, he appeared to be taking this best man thing seriously. Very seriously. It was . . . attractive, seeing him work hard at making his brother happy.

That night she watched from the sidelines as he ran the bachelor/bachelorette party like he'd been born a host, with natural charm and easy laughter.

And the way the others clearly loved him . . . It

made her happy to know that he'd made it, that he'd turned out okay and had so much love and light in his life.

Just as it made her feel slightly alone and a little . . . sad. Because she didn't have that. She had her mom. Her cousin Garrett McGrath. And a few good friends. But her relationships definitely seemed to fall a little short of what Sean had with this group of tight-knit family and friends.

Sunday morning, she woke up before dawn. There was so much to do. She made breakfast, telling herself she was relieved it was check-out day. Soon, Sean would march out of her life again and she'd go to Cabo and forget him.

Okay, so she'd never been able to forget him, but it was past time to learn.

Chapter Three

I⊤ wᴀꜱ barely dawn when Sean sat up in his bed and looked at his phone's notifications. *"Shit."*

The mound under the covers of the second bed moved. Groaned. Then Joe flopped to his back and gave Sean a bleary-eyed look. "Unless there are two really hot women at our door wanting to jump our bones, it's *way* too early to be up."

"The storm worsened," Sean said. "There's flooding and mudslides up and down the entire state of California. The roads in and out of here are closed."

"Then why the hell are you waking me up?"

"Because mudslides closed Finn and Pru's wedding venue down. Indefinitely."

"Okay, that sucks," Joe said on a wide yawn. "But I think the wedding panic can wait until daylight, yeah?" And without waiting for an answer, he rolled over and went back to sleep.

Sean dressed and went down the hall, knocking on the first guest room he came to. Tina opened the door. The six-foot-plus dark-skinned goddess was in only a towel, damp from the shower. Behind her, he could see both beds, one tousled but empty, the other holding a sleeping Kylie.

"What's up, Sugar?" Tina asked. "I'm halfway through applying my mascara and it's a process. I need to get back to it."

Sean repeated his spiel. "The storm worsened," he said. "There's mudslides everywhere between here and home. We're not getting out for a while."

Tina smiled. "A few extra days away from the city and work? Love it."

"The wedding venue closed."

"Well damn," Tina said. "But we'll help Pru and Finn figure it out. Later, when I have all my lashes on."

Behind Tina, Kylie sat up, looking confused. Her hair was rioted all around her head as she narrowed her eyes at Sean. "Why are you interrupting my beauty sleep?"

"The weather—"

"—Sean," she said, holding up a hand. "I love you. I do. But this bed's amazing. In fact, I plan to marry the next guy that makes me feel even half as good as this bed does. So please go away."

Sean moved to the next door. Neither Archer nor Elle bothered to answer to his knock so he texted Archer.

Sean: It's me. Open up.

Archer: Keep knocking and die. Painfully.

Okay then. Since Archer wasn't much of a joker, Sean kept moving. But at Spence and Colbie's room, it was more of the same, although they at least answered the door. Both had clearly been otherwise preoccupied. Spence told Sean not to expect him and Colbie until much, *much* later.

Giving up on riling anyone else up besides himself, Sean made his way downstairs. He sat at one of the three round dining room tables. The power had gone out again and stayed off this time, so the only light came from a few well-placed lanterns and candles. He checked his phone but nothing had changed.

They were still screwed.

In fact, most of Northern California was, and now also in a newly declared state of emergency. Overnight there'd been three inches of rain causing mudslides, sinkholes, and massive road closures. People couldn't get out of Napa Valley. And they couldn't get *into* Napa Valley—not that that mattered with the wedding venue closed down. It'd be months, their site said, before they recovered from the devastating mudslides and were operating again.

"It's a nightmare," Finn said, plopping down next to him. He had a plate full of food from the sideboard buffet.

Sean slid his gaze to his brother as he shoved in some French toast and bacon. "Real upset over it, are you?"

"Devastated," Finn said and craned his neck to

eyeball the food platters. "Think we can go back up there for seconds?"

"Are you serious?"

"Yeah. The French toast's amazing here. That innkeeper, Lotti? She's incredible. She's got a small generator and she used it to cook for us. Have you eaten yet?"

"No," Sean said. "I haven't. Because I've been sitting here trying to figure out how to save your wedding. Where's Pru?"

"She and the girls are about to go have mimosas in the thankfully gas-powered hot tub."

Sean stared at him. "Does she know about the flooding and mudslides closing down her wedding venue?"

"Yep."

"And she's okay?"

"No," Finn said. "Which is why she's inhaling alcohol at the asscrack of dawn. Listen, she's trying to have a good attitude about this and so am I." He shoved in more French toast. "She said as long as we're in the same place with the people we love, that's good enough. I have to believe her. She waited a long time for this and now there's nothing else open all year. We might have to hit up the courthouse to tie the knot and throw a party. Whatever she wants." Finn wolfed down the rest of his food and sighed, scrubbing a hand down his face, revealing his tension and stress.

For years the guy had been taking care of Sean.

When their parents had died, Sean had been a fourteen-year-old punk-ass kid, but Finn hadn't hesitated. At twenty-one, he'd stepped into the role of mom and dad and brother, and for a lot of days also judge and jury and jailer.

He'd never once failed Sean.

But Sean had failed Finn. Way too many times to count. He owed Finn everything, including the fact that he was even still here to tell the tale, because there'd been more than a few times where his stupidity should've gotten him killed.

And during that time, Finn hadn't once given up on him. He hadn't even let Sean see the strain it'd surely taken on his own life, taking care of a perpetually pissed-off-at-the-world teenager.

But this, today . . . it was a strain. It was in the tightness of Finn's shoulders and the grim set to his mouth.

His older brother wasn't okay.

And Sean was going to have his back, no matter what. He clasped a hand on Finn's shoulder. "I'm going to work this out for you guys," he said.

Finn smiled and shook his head. "Not your problem, man. Don't worry about it."

Something Finn had been saying to Sean since day one. *Don't worry about it, I'll handle it.* And he had. No matter what Sean had thrown at him.

Finn got to his feet.

"Where are you going?" Sean asked.

"To join my hopefully soon-to-be wife in the hot tub."

"Finn, we still have to check out of here this morning."

Finn shook his head. "You said it yourself, the roads are closed. We're not going anywhere."

"Did anyone actually check in with Lotti about the fact that we have to extend our stay?"

Finn stopped. "Shit. No."

"Don't worry about it," Sean said. "I'll handle it." And with that, he got up and moved out to the front room to deal with the problems for once.

There was no sign of Lotti at the front desk so he walked around it and peered into her office, hitting the jackpot.

Lotti was in the corner, sitting on top of a very overstuffed suitcase, bouncing up and down on it trying to get it closed while simultaneously listening to a call she had on speaker.

A female voice was saying ". . . I can't believe you talked me into this, a cruise through the Greek islands with Aunt Judie, but we're having a ball, honey. I just want you to remember your promise to me before I left, that you're going to use your honeymoon tickets and go to Cabo. You need a breather from the past year, first losing your daddy and then breaking off your wedding—"

"Mom." Lotti closed her eyes. "I'm fine."

"Are you?"

"Yes," Lotti said firmly. "I mean, I did wake up this morning to realize I'm still not a billionaire rock star rocket scientist martial arts master, but hey, it could be worse, right?"

"Honey. I worry about you. If you don't leave your past in the past, it'll destroy your future. You've got to live for what today's offering, not for what yesterday took away from you."

"You sound like a Hallmark card."

"They don't make cards for this, Lotti."

"I'm okay, Mom. Really," Lotti said firmly. "Tell me about you."

"Well . . . are you ready for this? I'm wearing sunscreen and a very cute new dress that I couldn't pair a bra with, and there's a gentleman who keeps sending me drinks. I think I'm about to have a very good time."

"Be safe," Lotti said softly. "Love you."

"Love you too!"

Lotti tapped the screen of her phone and disconnected. Then she looked down at the suitcase beneath her and sighed before going back to bouncing on it to try to get it zipped. "Come on you, fu—"

"Here," Sean said, coming into the office to crouch in front of her, taking over possession of the zipper. "Let me."

Lotti had gone Bambi in the headlights. "Where did you come from?" she asked.

"Well when a mommy and daddy love each other very much they—"

"Were you eavesdropping?" she demanded, not amused.

"No."

"So . . . you heard nothing?" she asked suspiciously. "Nothing at all?"

He lifted his attention from the suitcase that was not going to zip and met her gaze.

She searched his face and closed her eyes. "Dammit."

He put a hand on her leg. "I'm sorry—"

"No. You don't get to say that to me."

"I lost my dad too, Lotti. And my mom. No one understands how that feels except someone who's been through it."

She chewed on that for a minute. Trying to get her emotions under control, he realized.

"Are you also going to tell me that you've been dumped by a fiancé a week before your wedding?" she finally asked.

"Well no, but—

"No buts." She shoved his hand from her. "I don't want to talk about it."

"Lotti—"

"Ever," she said firmly. "New subject."

"Okay. How about the fact that there's no way your suitcase is going to close."

"Dammit." She hopped off the suitcase and kneeled in front of it, pulling out some of the clothes. "I tried to pack light. But it was hard to decide on what to wear . . ."

"Depends on what you want to get out of the trip," he said.

She bit her lower lip and blushed, and he went brows up. "Ah," he said. "You want to get laid."

"No," she said but even her ears were deep red now.

"Hey, there's nothing wrong with that," he said.

She met his eyes and then rolled hers. "Well gee, thanks for the permission." She pulled something else from her suitcase and held it up to herself. A white strappy sundress. "Would this dress make you want me?"

He had to laugh. "Lotti, when I first met you, you were in PE class wearing a baggy T-shirt and sweats and I wanted you."

"I'm being serious, Sean."

"So am I."

She shook her head. "Back then was a lot of years ago and I'm not that same skinny kid. Be honest, is the dress too much? I don't want to look desperate, even though I am."

"The dress is perfect," he said, not liking that she believed she needed the dress to attract a man. All she needed to do was lay those heart-stopping eyes on someone and it'd be over. All the rest; her smile, her brain, her bod . . . it was all gravy. "On second thought," he said and snatched the sundress and tossed it aside.

She snorted and tried again to get the zipper closed, bouncing up and down on the suitcase again. "Is this helping?"

Sean tried not to watch her lovely breasts jiggle and failed. "Helps a lot."

She followed his gaze to her chest and snorted again. "You're impossible."

He got the suitcase closed and rose to his feet to help her to hers. "Just trying to take your mind off your troubles." And he meant that. He wanted to take her mind off the phone call, something he himself couldn't do.

She'd been left by her fiancé.

Her dad had died.

And she'd needed this Cabo getaway more than he'd known. "I'm sorry about today, Lotti."

Startled, her dark eyes met his. "What about it?"

"Well, for starters, about us not checking out—"

"Oh, you don't have to check out," she said. "It's automatic. All you have to do is leave."

"Yeah, about that . . . Have you checked the news or weather?"

She stared at him and then shook her head. "Not yet. I got sidetracked trying to get my suitcase closed."

"We can't leave, Lotti."

"Sure you can," she said. "You just get in your vehicle and go." She gave him a little push toward the door for emphasis. "Okay, then. Thanks for coming, buh-bye . . ."

But Sean wasn't walking away. Not that this stopped her from trying to get him to. She put her hands on his chest and pushed again. It seemed to take her a second to realize that he wasn't going to be moved. Finally, she went hands on hips and gave him a long look. "You're leaving, and so am I. I've got big plans."

Yeah, he knew. Plans that had nearly involved the sexy white sundress he couldn't get his mind off of.

"I mean it," she said. "I'm heading straight to the airport and Cabo. So if you're about to give me any sort of news to the contrary, I don't want to hear it."

She was spoiling for a fight, but he wasn't going to give it to her, not with that vulnerable look on her face and his realization that she needed this getaway so much more than he'd even realized. "I'm sorry," he said quietly. "I really am. But you need to bring up your flight app. Or your weather or news app."

She looked out the window where the rain and wind had actually died down for the time being. "Why? What don't I know?"

"The highways are closed."

Her head whipped back to face him. "What?"

"Which means people can't get out," he said. "People like us. And you."

"No."

"Yes."

She stared at him and let out a long, shuddering breath. "Okay, you know what? After much consideration, I've decided adulthood isn't for me. Thank you and goodbye."

"I'm sorry, Lotti."

"No, you don't understand," she said. "I have flights."

"I know."

She looked around. "And I'm actually off work for once. There's no other guests until after the first of the year." She paused. "Are you sure there aren't any open roads out of here, not a single one?"

"Not until the storm moves on and they've cleared everything of debris. The reports say we're at least twenty-four hours out from that. More likely forty-eight hours, or even more."

"Oh my God." She sank heavily to her desk chair, dropping her forehead to the desk. "This is all my fault."

"Yeah? You personally called Mother Nature and asked her to unload her wrath?"

Keeping her head down, she moaned. "I actually thought this was going to happen, that I could get away from here. Two weeks, that's all I asked for."

"I'm so sorry your vacay got screwed up. And I'm sorry for my next question."

She lifted her head. Her smile faded. "Sean, you can't stay. I'm closing down the inn."

"That's already happened, Lotti," he said on a low laugh. "I hear you but there's literally nowhere to go."

With a sigh, she stood up and faced him. "Okay, then what's your question?"

"Since we're all stuck for at least the next twenty-four hours, I was hoping we could throw my brother and Pru an impromptu wedding reception."

"That's usually preceded by an actual wedding," she said.

"Yeah. Thought we could do that too."

She stared at him. "You've lost it."

"This place is actually the perfect wedding setting."

She laughed but when he didn't, she shook her

head. "Sean, a wedding is an organized event. I mean, I'm a very organized person. I have lists and check them twice and all that, but even I couldn't pull this off on the fly on my own, and I don't have any employees scheduled because I was supposed to be off work." She picked up a clipboard on her desk and showed him, flipping through all the stuff she had on it.

She was right, she was organized as hell. He stopped her on the page labeled: Cabo. There were three things listed:

Sand
Surf
Surfer

"That's my to do list for Cabo," she said. "Beneath it's my flight itinerary, which says nothing about being sidelined by the storm of the century."

He met her gaze, which was dialed to stubborn and determined. And . . . hopeful. "Your to do list includes a surfer?" he asked.

She looked a little embarrassed but held his gaze. "I've discovered that I've got a little problem with relationships," she said. "So I'm trying something new. I'm going for the *opposite* of a relationship. And nothing, not the storm, not my B&B responsibilities, not even you is going to stop me."

"I can appreciate that," he said. "But—"

"No buts, Sean. I don't have time for buts. And here, let me make you another list, one of everything else I don't have time for." She grabbed a pen and hurriedly scribbled on a piece of paper, which she handed to him.

Things I don't have time for:
1. Your shit
2. Crazy shit
3. Bullshit
4. Stupid shit
5. Fake shit
6. Shit that has nothing to do with me

He laughed, thinking his younger self had been the biggest idiot on the planet that he'd let her get away. She was funny, sweet, amazing, and sexy as hell. "I get it," he said. "But sometimes life doesn't play along. We're not getting out of here and neither are you."

"Dammit," she said.

"So . . . about having a wedding here . . ."

"Seriously, you're nuts."

Yeah. There was no doubt. And something else. He couldn't stop looking at her. For him, she was everything he'd never deserved, especially all those years ago. He should've left things alone, left their attraction as a "what if." But he'd never been good at leaving things alone. He hadn't been able to resist taking a taste of her, even though he'd not been mature enough for her. He'd had issues over losing people, big issues.

So when she'd told him that she was moving,

he'd simply walked away first. Yeah, he'd been a first-rate asshole, but the truth was he always walked first to protect himself.

Except now the joke was on him because even to this very day, she was still the one who'd gotten away. And as a result of what he'd done, Lotti now walked away from relationships, at least emotionally, because she was afraid of getting hurt and he hated that. "It's not *completely* nuts," he said. "I could get ordained online and—"

"Sean," she said on a low laugh. "It won't work. There's not enough room, for one thing. And there's no one to cater. No wedding decorations or cake or—"

"The big living room is perfect," he said. "We all fit in it, no problems. And you won't have to do a thing, I'll handle it all."

She just stared at him. "That doesn't sound like you."

He managed a small smile. "People change, Lotti. I've changed."

"So you keep saying," she said softly and paused. "Look, I think it's incredibly sweet of you to want to do this for your brother. You're trying to make up for your past."

He held her gaze. "Yes. Apparently, I have a lot to make up for."

She flushed a pretty pink and lifted a shoulder.

"Oh, don't go shy on me now," he said with a smile. "I still need to hear specifics on the 'not that great' thing."

She covered her face.

He felt a ping in his heart. "I really was that bad, huh?" he said as lightly as he could.

"Well, it's not like I'm keeping score or anything," she murmured demurely.

"But . . ." he coaxed, giving her a "go on" gesture with his hand.

"Okay, okay, but remember you asked." She hesitated. "Everything was actually great, but only one of us . . . finished."

He winced at his own ineptitude back then but managed to catch her when she laughed and went to turn away. "If I could go back," he said solemnly, "and do things differently, I would."

This clearly surprised her. "You would?"

"One hundred percent." He paused. "I'd like a chance to right my wrongs with you, Lotti. *All* of them."

She stared up at him as if she wanted to believe that and he leaned in, letting their bodies touch, and when her breath caught, he felt a surge of relief.

He wasn't in this alone. She still felt something for him, even if she didn't know what exactly.

"I think you'll be too busy to right that particular wrong," she said a little breathlessly, not moving away, but instead making sure they stayed plastered up against each other.

He stared down at her mouth and wanted it on his. So badly that he lost track of what she was saying. "Too busy doing what?"

"Giving your brother a wedding."

"Wait." He stilled. "You're in?"

"Well far be it for me to be the one who stands in the way of you doing something amazing for your brother," she said. "Besides, what do you know about planning a wedding?"

"Uh . . ."

"Exactly," she said. "I'm going to go out on a limb here and guess that you know *nothing* about it. Whereas I know more than you, at least. So . . ."

"So . . ." He took her hand in his. "We're doing this."

She inhaled a deep breath and let it out slowly as she squeezed his hand. "I guess I'm nuts too, but yeah, we're doing this."

Chapter Four

L︎OTTI WAS pretty good at picking herself back up after a fall, proverbial or otherwise. She'd had to be. By late afternoon, the storm had renewed itself and she'd resigned herself to that, and also to playing hostess for longer than she'd intended. And if she was being honest, it wasn't exactly a hardship to get an extra day or two with Sean in the house.

Darkness came quick at this time of year. In one blink, the gray and stormy day turned to a pitch black stormy night. Electricity had come and gone several times.

They were all pretty much used to it by now.

Lotti had spent several hours with everyone, going over what they could do to make a wedding actually work. Lotti had been pleasantly surprised to find Pru a very calm, logical, easy to please bride-to-be. Sean's brother, Finn, was pretty great too. He just wanted to make Pru happy.

The rest of the friends were . . . well, amazing. Flexible. Loving. Sarcastic. Lotti loved them all. They'd decided on the next day for the ceremony and were making lists for the plans.

"I'm so excited we're going to do this here," Pru's friend Willa said. "It was going to be a 'rustic Christmas' wedding at the winery, but this here . . ." She gestured to the holiday-decoration-strewn place. "This is the real deal rustic. And also, you're wonderful, Lotti. And you too, Pru. If the weather had messed up *my* wedding, I'd probably be acting like an angel who'd just had their wings broken."

"We're *all* angels," Elle, another bridesmaid, said. "And when someone breaks our wings, we simply continue to fly . . . on a broomstick. We're flexible like that."

"We're extremely limited in food and resources," Lotti warned. "I was expecting to close up today for several weeks so supplies are almost nonexistent."

Finn looked worried about this. "You mean food? We're short food?"

Pru, sitting next to him, raised a brow. "Since when do we need food to get married?"

"We need sustenance, that's all I'm saying. Maybe—"

"Hold on." Pru gave him a long look. "If you're trying to say you don't want to do this after talking me into it, then let me be clear and say that I *will* run you through with my umbrella while you sleep."

Finn blinked. "That was oddly specific and violent."

"I stand by my statement," Pru said.

Finn eyed said umbrella and nudged it farther away from her.

Pru laughed before looking around the room at her friends, all of whom were sitting around, taking part in this emergency wedding meeting. "I know we could wait," she said. "I could start all over with a new venue, but . . . I don't want to." She reached for Finn's hand. "Everyone we love and need is right here. I want to do this. Here."

Finn leaned over, and apparently not at all concerned about their audience, kissed her softly. He stayed close, their gazes connected for a long beat during which their love seemed to fill the room.

It was so . . . *real* that Lotti actually had to look away. She'd never experienced anything like what the two of them shared, had never in her life yearned that much for one person. Her gaze collided with Sean's and her heart skipped a beat. Okay, so she had felt that way. Once. But she'd been young and stupid. It'd been puppy love, clearly not anything like what Pru and Finn so clearly had. But now she could admit that after only a few days with Sean as an adult, he was even more appealing than he'd been all those years ago and looking into his green eyes, she saw emotion there, deep emotion.

I want a chance to right my wrongs with you, Lotti. All of them.

Damn but he still could still reach her. In the gut. In her overactive brain. And the hardest hit was . . . right in her heart, and she had to close her eyes and remind herself she no longer was interested in such things. Not even a little bit. She'd already planned to go the opposite route from here on out and she needed to stick with that. Sun, surf, surfer.

She realized everyone was looking at her and that Pru had asked a question. "I'm sorry," she said. "What did you say?"

"I just wanted to make sure you're really okay with all this," Pru said. "It's asking an awful lot of you. We're of course going to pay for everything; the extra stay, your time, your resources, all of it. But . . . are you really okay with us pretty much hi-jacking your B&B and turning it into a wedding site?"

"Of course," Lotti said with much more ease than she felt, avoiding Sean's gaze because he seemed to still be able to read her like a book. "We're already halfway there."

Pru nodded and reached over and hugged her. "Thank you."

"What will you wear?" Elle asked.

Pru's smile fell a bit. "Oh crap. I don't have a dress. I never even thought of that."

"I have a dress," Lotti said and when everyone looked at her, she lifted a shoulder. "Don't worry, it was never worn. We've done weddings here before, in the backyard. There's also a pretty wooden archway in the shed out back. And I have those beautiful potted flowers in the dining room and foyer. We can rearrange them in here to make an aisle."

Everyone was looking at her in awe like she was

some sort of creative genius. But she wasn't. Not even close. It'd all been for *her* wedding, the one that hadn't actually happened. But hell, it might as well all go to some good, right?

Right.

By that night, Lotti was looking down at her clipboard thinking they might actually pull this off. The property next door belonged to a rancher who'd been the son of her dad's best friend. Jack told her to send someone over, that he could help with extra provisions. On the far side of him was another neighbor, Sally, a close friend who ran a garden nursery. She said she didn't have much in the way of blooming flowers at this time of year but to come over and help themselves.

Lotti had sent the guys to the ranch and the ladies to the nursery. Everyone came back wet but the men had three frozen pizzas, a package of bacon, and the makings for tacos. Lotti slid a worried look to Pru on the items but she seemed on board.

"I know some people are all about live, laugh, love," Pru said. "But I'm all about pizza, bacon, and tacos."

During the cleaning and straightening and planning melee, Lotti's mom called to check on her since she'd seen the weather on the news. Lotti had told her she was fine, she still had guests and was working.

Her mom had paused. "Anyone single and gainfully employed and worth going for?"

Lotti had rolled her eyes and then rushed her off

the phone before being dragged into that conversation, because her mom had *nothing* on the CIA. She could sniff out a secret from five thousand miles no problem.

Not ten minutes later, Lotti's phone buzzed an incoming text from her cousin Garrett.

Garrett: You didn't get to Cabo.

Lotti: Mom's such a tattletale. Weather's bad.

Garrett: She didn't say anything about the weather.
She had hopes you were with a guy.

Lotti: Is there a point to this conversation?

Garrett: Just remember, if his name starts with A-Z,
he's likely to ruin your life. You were warned.

Lotti had to laugh, but she put her phone away and her family out of her mind. That night, they all shared the pizzas, saving the bacon for the morning and the tacos for the wedding feast. Afterward, everyone went to bed early.

With the storm still battering the poor house, Lotti stood in the living room and took in the big picture windows and wide open wooden staircase, knowing that it'd make a beautiful spot for a wedding. One that would actually happen . . .

She drew in a deep breath and wondered what

had come over her to agree to such madness. She had no idea.

Except she did. In spite of herself and the things she'd been through, she still believed in love.

And . . . she wasn't quite ready to have Sean walk away. Not yet. The thought gave her a hot flash. Needing some fresh air, she walked through the kitchen and stepped out the back door, stopping under the roof overhang, listening to the rain fall as she took in the view of the valley. Dressed in a light sweater, skirt, and tights, she wasn't exactly prepared for the weather but she didn't care.

A few minutes later, someone joined her on the patio.

Sean.

He met her gaze, studied her face as if he was making sure she was okay, and when he realized she was, he gave her a small smile. They stood there together, neither speaking, standing side by side as the rain fell. When their fingers brushed against each other, Sean turned his hand, touching his palm to hers, entwining their fingers.

"You were amazing today," he said. "I can't believe how you put an entire wedding together in one day."

She shrugged, hoping to keep her secrets to herself. She felt the weight of Sean's gaze on her face and she closed her eyes so he couldn't catch her thoughts like only he seemed to be able to do, but she was too late.

"Lotti," he said softly. Just that. Just her name, with a whole lot of feeling in it.

Shit. He knew. She swallowed hard and stared out into the night—until he turned her to face him.

"Lotti," he said again, that same level of emotion in his voice.

"Don't," she whispered.

"I'm sorry," he said huskily. "I should've seen it earlier. All this . . . it was for your wedding."

"Well not the pizzas."

He didn't smile. "I hate that I put you in this position. It's not too late, Lotti. You don't have to do this."

"It's okay. Really." She closed her eyes. "But I'd like to be alone now."

"I get that, and I'd really like to give you what you want," he said. "But I can't. Not this time."

Chapter Five

AT THE empathetic tone in Sean's voice, Lotti's heart and stomach and head all clenched in unison. "What do you mean you can't give me what I want?" she asked. "All you have to do is walk away."

"Tried that already," he said. "And it was the biggest mistake of my life." He brought her hand up to his mouth and met her gaze over their entwined hands.

He was looking at her like . . . well, she wasn't sure what was going on in his head, but *her* thoughts were racing along with her pulse.

"You're incredible, Lotti. I hope you know that." Very slowly, clearly giving her time to object, he pulled her into him.

Her breath caught at the connection and his eyes heated in response as he slid a hand up her spine and then back down again, pressing her in tight to him from chest to thighs and everywhere in between. His nose was cold at the crook of her neck, but his breath was warm against her skin. She felt his lips press against the sensitive spot just behind her ear and she shivered. "You're trembling," he said, his voice low. "Are you cold?"

"No," she whispered. Try the opposite of cold . . .

"Nervous?"

"No." Not even close. The way his mouth moved across her skin was making her warm all over. Not that she could articulate that with his body pressed to hers and his fingers dancing over her skin. She was literally quivering as the memories of what it felt like to be touched by him washed over her, as if no time at all had gone by.

Yes, she'd let him think that their time together had sucked for her. But it hadn't. Not even close. That long-ago night he'd evoked feelings and a hunger in her that she'd never forgotten. "I've just had a long day," she said.

"I know. I'm going to make it better." He pressed a kiss at the juncture of her jaw and ear before he made his way to her lips for a slow, hot kiss, his mouth both familiar and yet somehow brand-new. She was so far gone that when he pulled back she protested with a moan, but he held her tight, staring down at her with heated eyes. "Just checking," he murmured.

"Checking what?"

"That you want this as badly as I do."

She sure as hell hadn't meant to want him at all, but she fisted her hands in his shirt and yanked him back in. When he let out a soft laugh, she kissed him to shut him up. She shut herself up too as she lost herself in his kiss, in his touch as their hands grappled to get on each other, touching, caressing, possessing.

She'd have denied this until her dying day, but God she'd missed this, missed the feel of his mouth on hers, missed his hands on her body, missed *him*.

But she was no longer a clueless teenager, and neither was Sean. They were grownups with entirely different lives from each other. "I can't," she whispered and slowly opened her eyes to face his.

"Can't?" he asked. "Or not interested?"

She hesitated, but then gave a slow shake of her head. "Not interested."

Sean gave her fingers—the ones she'd dug into his biceps—a wry look.

She quickly dropped her hands. Okay, fine. She was interested. So very interested. And also dying of curiosity. Would this time feel different?

"I've changed," he promised her. "Give me a chance, Lotti. Give us a chance."

Unable to help herself, she touched his jaw, letting her fingers slide into his silky hair and for a beat, pressed close to him again. It'd be so easy to fall for him. *Too* easy. And knowing it, she stepped back. "I've changed too," she said. "No more relationships for me. They don't work out."

"How many?"

She blinked. "How many what?"

"How many relationships haven't worked out?" he asked.

"Two, an ex-boyfriend and ex-fiancé."

"You're not counting me?"

"Hard to count someone you only got naked with one time."

He paused and then laughed softly. Mad, she turned away to go back inside but he caught her and pulled her around. He'd stopped laughing, which meant she didn't have to kill him outright, but he was still smiling.

"I don't appreciate you laughing at me," she said stiffly.

"I'm not laughing at you," he said. "You're amazing. I'm laughing at myself. We've *both* been relationship shy. You, because I hurt you. Me, because I'm the idiot who hurt you. Please give me another chance, Lotti."

She shook her head. "No. I'm over that. I'm going to Cabo to drink fancy cocktails and smell like coconut sunscreen and to have a one-night stand with *no* strings."

He stared down into her eyes, no longer laughing. Or smiling. "I know I have no right to ask, but do you trust me, even a little?"

"I don't know." She stared at him right back. "Maybe a very little tiny spark."

"I'll take that." He gave her a quick kiss that was no less heart-stopping than his previous one. "Give me fifteen minutes. I'll meet you at your apartment."

"For what?"

But he was already gone.

You're not going to do it, she told herself. No way. She hadn't been expecting him. At all. In fact, many times over the years she'd told herself to forget him.

But she hadn't. Not even a little bit.

Chapter Six

Fifteen minutes later Lotti climbed the stairs to her apartment.

"You're late!" Peaches yelled as she entered.

She ignored the parrot for a moment, Sean's earlier words floating in her brain.

Do you trust me, even just a little?

She still wasn't sure but her apartment was lit with candles flickering on every surface. He'd somehow come up with two large cutouts of palm trees, which were on either side of her bed. There were blue and green scarves on top of her lampshades, giving the entire place the feel of . . . water.

Sean stood in the center of the room wearing board shorts and a T-shirt that advertised some surf shop in Mexico. No shoes and a pair of sunglasses shoved up on his head. He was holding a pitcher of what looked like strawberry margaritas and a bottle of coconut suntan oil.

"What's all this?" she asked.

"Take out the trash!" Peaches yelled.

Sean slid a look at the parrot. "We discussed

this," he told the bird. "You were going to let me do the talking."

"All you want is sex!" Peaches squeaked. "I need it to mean something!"

Lotti strode across the room, took a blue silk scarf off one of the lamps, and covered Peaches's cage. "Say goodnight, Peaches."

"Goodnight, Peaches," Peaches muttered and huffed out a sigh.

Lotti turned to Sean, who was laughing. "I didn't train him," she said. "My dad did. He wanted to drive my mom crazy." She took in the room and realized he'd incorporated everything she'd had on her clipboard. Sand, surf . . . surfer. And he was most definitely the hottest surfer she'd ever seen. "What is all this, Sean?"

"Since you can't get to Mexico, I brought Mexico to you."

"How did you accomplish all this in fifteen minutes?"

"Maybe you're not the only one with the taking care of everyone else skill." He lifted a shoulder with a little self-deprecating grimace. "Mine, of course, is a newer skill, so I'm not sure how I'm doing."

Her heart squeezed. "You're doing amazing." And because the answering look he gave her had more than her heart reacting, she went for a distraction. "Tell me that's strawberry margaritas."

"It is. And I didn't do this alone. I had help. Elle, Pru, Willa, and Colbie are real good in a pinch. Especially Elle. She's a miracle maker. We're not even sure she's human." He poured them each a glass— hers had a little umbrella in it. He gently clicked his drink to hers. "To Mexico."

She drank to that and then rolled her sore neck.

He gently took her glass and set it on her night- stand. "Take off your sweater and lie down," he said. "On your front."

She went brows up. "I don't think I've had enough tequila yet."

"I'm going to use the suntan oil for all your kinks."

Her breath stuttered in her throat as all sorts of dirty, wicked images floated in her head.

". . . In your neck," he said with a smile that said he knew exactly where her mind had gone.

She'd reached for her drink and taken a big sip when he'd said "kinks," and she nearly snorted te- quila out her nose. "I'm not losing my top before you do," she wheezed.

Without a word, he pulled his T-shirt off and let it hit the floor. He stood there looking comfortable as hell in nothing but those board shorts riding low on his hips, revealing proof that the lean, lanky boy was now all man. Still lean but oh so many mus- cles, each delineated in a way that was making her mouth water. She took another gulp of her liquid courage. "You really think I'm just going to strip?"

"That would be my greatest fantasy, but all I asked for was your sweater."

She took another long sip of her margarita.

"Okay," she said, staring at his chest, the one she wanted to lick like a lollipop from his chin to waistband of those shorts and beyond. "Just my sweater." But she didn't move.

He smiled. "It's not like I haven't seen it all before."

"Hey, that was a long time ago!"

He cocked his head, looking her over. "Has anything changed?"

"No." Well, maybe a little. She wasn't as skinny as she'd been, for one thing. "Maybe," she admitted.

"I'll close my eyes."

She snorted again and pulled off her top. Beneath she was wearing a plain black sports bra. Not exactly sexy since it had more coverage than a bathing suit top would've provided. Feeling safe, she climbed up on her bed and lay facedown. "Do your worst."

The scent of coconut hit her just before his warm hands did. Coated in oil, they glided firmly up her back and she let out a shuddery moan of pleasure before she could stop herself.

It'd been so long since someone had touched her . . . too long. She wanted him to keep going, wanted him to touch every inch of her and remind her what she'd been missing.

She felt the depression of the mattress when Sean got onto the bed and straddled her for a better reach. Then his amazing hands went to work kneading the knots in her shoulders and neck, and she moaned again.

"You're a mess, baby," he murmured, his fingers tangling with her sports bra.

She *was* a mess and in far more ways than one. Reaching back, she unhooked the bra's three hooks and Sean stilled.

Buoyed by that, Lotti went through the acrobatic motions of carefully pulling her arms out of the loops without revealing too much or showing him her face, which she knew would've been the biggest reveal of all. She was sure her need and hunger was all over it.

"Lotti." Sean's voice sounded strained, husky, and she felt herself go damp in response.

"Wouldn't want to get funny tan lines," she said.

He let out a low half laugh, half groan, and then his weight shifted. "Tan lines are a bitch," he agreed. He was at her side again, this time so his hands could glide beneath her skirt. He got ahold of her tights and slid them down her legs, dropping them to the floor.

Now *she* was the one to freeze. Not because she wanted him to stop but because she was afraid he *would* stop. She felt his coconut oiled hands on her legs now, massaging his way up from the balls of her feet to the backs of her thighs, just under the edge of her skirt.

"Lotti?" he asked, voice gruff.

She had to clear her throat to speak. "Yeah?"

"How do you feel about tan lines on your ass?"

"Hate them," she said.

Her skirt was gone before she could blink. By

some miracle, she was wearing her favorite pair of purple bikini bottoms.

"Pretty," he murmured. "But they've got to go too." And then he hooked his thumbs on either side and slowly pulled them down. They hit the floor by her skirt and she held her breath.

As if she wasn't laid out before him like some sort of feast, he started at the bottom of her feet again, slowly working his strong fingers over the tense muscles. Her calves. The backs of her thighs. Her lower back. Her upper back, shoulders, and neck. Her arms, all the way down to her fingers. And then finally, he made his way down her spine to her ass.

Until now, he'd been silent, giving her the best massage of her entire life. If she hadn't been so unbearably aroused, she might have fallen asleep. But as he went along, he mixed in a series of knowing touches that had her on the very edge. He stroked the tips of his fingers along her ribs and the sides of her breasts, the tops of the back of her thighs, making sure to graze her butt here and there too.

When he cupped a cheek in each of his big palms and squeezed, kneading, spreading her open, he let out a rough groan at the view he gave himself.

"Spread your legs, baby," he said softly, and then did it himself. With a hand on each of her ankles, he nudged her legs apart. Then he was between them, going back to massaging her again while she writhed helplessly beneath him, so unbearably aroused she couldn't lie still. Her nipples rubbed against her blanket, the same blanket that was balled up at the vee of her thighs, teasing her halfway to an orgasm. "Sean—"

"Turn over," he said, his voice giving her a full body shiver, which was when she realized it wasn't the blankets at all. It was 100 percent him.

Chapter Seven

LOTTI HAD a choice. Call this off now, or turn over and take what she wanted—which happened to be one sexy as hell Sean O'Riley.

She turned over.

Sean's dark eyes went molten lava and his breath caught audibly. "You're the most beautiful thing I've ever seen," he said and it was crazy. Just his words now, with neither of his hands on her, had her squirming.

In the ambient lighting he'd created, he looked like a pagan god, leaning over her in nothing but those board shorts, now so low on his lean hips as to be nearly indecent. She'd never seen anything sexier in her entire life. Catching her staring, he smiled and went to pour more oil on his hands but she shook her head.

"One of us is overdressed," she murmured.

Setting down the oil, he rose and unfastened his board shorts. Letting them fall, he kicked them off.

He'd gone commando and was aroused. Very aroused. She moistened her dry lips and said, "I'm glad I'm not on curfew this time. I don't think I can take another interruption."

Another low laugh left him. "Not going to happen." He bent his head and kissed her deeply, thoroughly, until she was writhing on the bed needing more. Reaching down, she wrapped her fingers around him and stroked, coaxing a deliciously male sound from his throat.

"You taste like a strawberry margarita," she murmured.

"I want to find out what you taste like," he said and slid down her body, kissing every inch of her as he went. Her jaw, her throat, her shoulder and collarbone. Her breasts. He spent long moments there, teasing, biting softly down on a nipple before drawing it into his mouth and sucking so that she arched off the bed.

"Mmm," he said, his voice low and hot. "You taste amazing." He nibbled a hip. Scraped his teeth over her belly, an inner thigh. Then the other.

And then in between.

She would've come right off the mattress if he hadn't had a hand on either of her hips holding her down, anchoring her to the bed as he had his merry way with her. Her entire body was tensed like a tightly coiled spring ready to snap and just when she thought she couldn't take any more, he slowed down and let her catch her breath.

Then he started over, again taking her to the very edge and holding her there until she was rocking mindlessly, her hands fisted in his hair, shamelessly begging for him to finish her.

Which he did.

Twice.

When he finally crawled back up her body, he kissed her before rolling on a condom while she watched—which was shockingly, incredibly arousing all by itself—and when he was done, his gaze swept over her as he gave himself a long, slow stroke.

Sitting up, she nudged his hands away and took over. His head fell back as a rough groan escaped him. When she leaned forward and licked his nipple in tune to another stroke, he wrapped an arm low around her hips and lifted her, guiding himself home.

He sank in deep. So deep she cried out his name and clutched at him. "Okay?" he asked, holding himself utterly still, the strain of doing so in every line of his gorgeous, hard body. "Do you want to stop?"

"Stop and I'll kill you, right here in Mexico where I could probably even get away with it."

His laugh was rough, as was hers. The sound must have triggered something inside him because he laid her back on the mattress, leaned over her, and drove into her, thrusting long and hard and deep. She wrapped her legs around his waist and met him stroke for stroke, crying out as he took her to paradise.

Sean might as well have just been hit by a run-away Mack truck. He felt that gobsmacked by what had just happened between him and Lotti. It'd been . . . incredible. Like holy shit, off the rails, into the stratosphere incredible. He glanced over at her and found her eyes closed. She was breathing like she'd just run a mile. Her skin was flushed and she was damp with sweat, her hair rioting wildly around her face. She looked thoroughly fucked and thoroughly sated.

And she'd never looked more beautiful. "Lotti."

She opened her eyes. They were dazed and glossy and unfocused. "Hmm?"

He rose up on an elbow and leaned over her. "Tell me that was real. That you didn't . . ."

Her eyes narrowed. "Didn't what?"

"Fake it."

She blinked and then . . . laughed. She laughed so hard that she started to choke and he had to yank her upright and get her some water, which she proceeded to *also* choke on.

It was an excruciating five minutes later before she could talk and he was waiting with a barely tethered impatience.

"You think I faked it?" she asked incredulously. "Twice?"

"Three times," he said.

She blushed a little, but overall looked so pleased with herself that he relaxed.

"Okay then," he said. "So you didn't."

"Wait a minute," she said. "What if I had? What then?"

"We'd start over from the beginning."

She stared at him and then gave a slow, sexy smile, and he felt his heart roll over and expose its underbelly.

"Then I definitely faked them," she said and lay back. "So you'd better start over from the beginning."

LYING there with Sean after round two, waiting for their heart rates to recover from stroke level, Lotti kept expecting him to get up and leave.

But he didn't.

Instead, he straightened the covers that they'd destroyed and then climbed back in bed with her.

"What are you doing?" she asked as he pulled her in close.

"Worried?" he asked.

When was he going to learn—she was *always* worried. Although a good amount of that worry faded, replaced by something else as he nuzzled at her jaw, making a very male, very sexy satisfied sound deep in his throat. "Are you . . . cuddling me?" she asked.

"Trying," he said, sounding amused.

She allowed it because who the hell was she kidding, she loved the way he was holding her, loved the feel of his warm, strong body cradling hers.

But she did feel that she needed to remind them both of something. "You know that what happens in Mexico stays in Mexico, right?"

"Sure," he said.

She opened her mouth to say "no *really*," but he stroked her hair from her face and smiled at her. "Not a cuddler, huh?"

"I like affection," she admitted. *Way too much.* "But you should know, I'm kind of . . . well, emotionally unavailable."

"Is that right?"

"Yes."

"And what does that mean exactly, 'kind of emotionally unavailable'?" he asked, looking sincerely interested, so she gave him the truth.

"It means I like it when you hold me," she said. "But I don't really want to answer any questions. Or talk," she added, wanting to cover all her bases.

He grinned and kissed her. "Maybe I'll wear you down."

Her biggest fear was that he already had. "Don't count on it."

"Okay, tough girl," he said softly, nuzzling at her throat. "No questions. No talking. You go ahead and give ignoring what's still between us your best shot. I'll wait right here."

Much later Lotti came awake suddenly. The last thing she remembered was . . . well, riding Sean like a wild bronco. But she was alone in her bed.

So he'd left after all.

Okay, she got it. She really did. But wait a minute. There was a dim light coming from the direction of her kitchen table.

Sean sat at it, working on his tablet. "Sorry," he said. "Did I wake you?"

"No." Realizing she was bare-ass naked, she grabbed the sheet and pulled it to her chin.

This made him smile. He was sitting on one of her chairs, which he'd turned around so his chest was leaning into the back of it, wearing nothing but those sexy as hell board shorts.

"What are you doing?" she asked.

"I just got ordained online."

She blinked.

"To marry Finn and Pru," he said. "Now I'm writing the ceremony. Or trying." He ran a hand down his face, making her take a closer look at him.

He looked . . . exhausted. And tense with stress.

She carefully slid out of the bed, keeping the sheet wrapped around her as she did. Moving to stand behind him, she leaned over his shoulder to look at his screen, but he cleared it.

"You're embarrassed," she said in surprise.

He grimaced. "Let's just say talking about love and commitment is new for me. Very new." Reaching back, he hooked an arm around her hips to keep her close.

"You're having regrets," she murmured, and utterly unable to help herself, slid her hands to his broad, bare shoulders.

He moaned and leaned into her fingers as they dug into his tense muscles. "Regrets, yes. Lots of them, actually," he said.

This had her freezing. She went to remove her hands from him, but he reached up and entwined their fingers, giving a little tug so that she leaned over him. Turning his head, he looked into her eyes as he lifted her hand to his mouth and brushed his lips across her palm. "Not about last night, Lotti. I have no regrets there. Not a single one."

She let out a breath she hadn't realized she'd been holding. She didn't have regrets either. What had happened between them had been . . . amazing. And it'd also told her something she'd already known about herself but hadn't accepted.

Regardless of how much time had gone by, regardless of her cocky talk of being emotionally unavailable, she was still greatly, deeply emotionally invested in Sean O'Riley. "If it's not me, what are you regretting?" she asked.

He gently squeezed her fingers. "How I handled things with you all those years ago. What a shithead I was in general." He pushed his tablet away. "That I can't pay my brother back for all he's done for me."

She shouldn't have felt surprised. Even after what had happened between her and Sean that long-ago night, she'd still known he was a good guy. But now, seeing the man he'd turned into, how he'd shed the anger and resentment and his adolescence and had gotten himself a life, a good one, warmed her. "It sounds to me as if you've been doing just that," she said, "paying him back, and have been for a few years now. You work with him running the pub. In fact, it sounds like you take care of him every bit as much as he ever took care of you."

He started to shake his head, and she leaned in and gave him a soft kiss. "Sean, I'm watching you work your ass off to give him the wedding he deserves. You're doing everything in your power to give it to him because you love him. It's . . ."

"What?"

"Moving," she said.

He turned around to face her and pulled her into his lap, running a hand through her hair, tucking it all back behind her ear. His knuckles slid along the outer shell and she suppressed a shiver of desire that slid slowly down her spine.

Brushing a soft kiss against her temple, he wrapped his arms around her and pressed his face into her throat. "I thought coming to Napa was such a mistake," he said. "I wanted to take everyone to Vegas for the weekend. Looking back, I can't believe how close I came to never running into you again."

She was quiet a moment, thinking about that. "I'm glad you came here," she finally admitted.

He squeezed her tight. "Me too."

They sat there together quietly, and she relaxed into him. "Show me?" she murmured, gesturing to the tablet.

He hesitated and then brought his screen up.

She stared at it in confusion. "It's . . ."

"Blank?" he asked. "Yeah." He huffed out a sigh. "I keep deleting everything I come up with."

"Why?"

"Because when it comes right down to it, I don't know shit about everlasting love."

"I've seen you with your friends, Sean. I've seen you with Finn. You're a very tight-knit group and you seem to be an important part of it. They all love you, especially your brother."

He didn't say anything to this but he did meet her gaze, his own revealing a vulnerability that reminded her of the younger Sean. "Tell me some of the things you've written and deleted," she said.

He looked away from her, facing the blank screen. "They're two of the strongest people I've ever met. They had to be. They each suffered some pretty big losses early on, which left them no choice but to pick themselves up and carry on." He paused. "That they found each other is a miracle. Neither of them were exactly open to the idea of love." He paused again and still she didn't speak, not wanting to interrupt him, but also unbearably moved.

"It wasn't love at first sight," Sean said quietly. "But I think that's the point. First, they had to learn to like each other. And then trust each other." His voice was a little thick. Gruff. "Love born of that, trust, is an everlasting kind of love."

Lotti's throat was tight with emotion. She still didn't speak because now she literally couldn't.

Sean sighed and nuzzled his jaw to hers. "You can see why I'm having trouble."

"No." Cupping his face, she lifted it and looked into his eyes, letting him see the emotion in hers. "It's incredible, Sean. You're incredible."

He closed his eyes and shook his head so she whispered it again against his stubble-roughened jaw. And then yet again against his mouth.

His arms came around her hard. "Careful," he murmured huskily, eyes still closed. "Our positions are reversed this time. After last night and this morning—and though the sex was amazing, that's not what I'm referring to—*you're* going to leave *me* with the broken heart." He opened his eyes and unerringly leveled her with his stark gaze.

She stared at him right back. "Don't tease me," she whispered.

"I'm not teasing."

And indeed, there was no light of joviality in his expression, not a drop, and she swallowed hard. "I didn't sleep with you to get back at you, Sean."

"No, you slept with me because you wanted a one-night stand with a surfer." A ghost of a smile crossed his lips. "Mission accomplished."

"Okay, so we know why I slept with you," she said. "But why did you sleep with me?"

He held her gaze. "Maybe I thought you might fall for me again and I'd get it right this time."

Her heart squeezed. "Sean—"

He put a finger to her lips. "Don't burst my bubble yet," he said and slowly fisted his hands in her hair, carefully pulling her in so that they shared their next breath of air. "Not until I'm finished giving you everything I've got."

"How much more could you possibly have?" she asked, shifting in his lap, humming in pleasure at what she found. "Wait. You don't need to tell me, I think I've just found out for myself."

With a snort, he rose from the chair in one easy movement, her still in his arms. He turned to the bed and tossed her onto it, retaining his grip on the sheet wrapped around her.

This meant she landed butt naked in the middle of the mattress. She bounced and let out a squeak, trying to roll over and grab the covers.

But Sean was quicker, snatching the blanket, dropping it on the floor behind him, along with the sheet.

His smile was badass wicked and filled with trouble as he put a knee on the bed and began to crawl toward her with nefarious intent in his sharp gaze.

With another squeak, she started to scramble to the edge of the bed but then stopped. What was she doing? She *wanted* him to catch her. So she waited until he was close and then *she* pounced on *him*, pushing him down to the bed and claiming the victor's spot.

His hands at her hips, he smiled up at her. "You think you've got me?"

She took his hands in hers and flattened them

above his head, stretching herself along the length of him. Still holding him down, her gaze locked on his, she lifted up and took him inside her body. "I know I do."

"Oh fuck, Lotti." He arched up into her, his neck corded, his face a mask of intense pleasure. "You do, you've got me. Do with me whatever you want."

So she did.

Chapter Eight

A FEW hours later, Sean stood in the large living room of the B&B, taking in the room with a narrowed eye. Christmas on crack, check. Candles everywhere, check. Chairs pulled from every room in the house arranged with an aisle for Pru to walk toward Finn, check. Music softly playing from a wireless speaker that was Bluetoothed to his phone, check.

There was no electricity, but they didn't need it. Outside, rain drummed steadily against the old Victorian, adding to the ambiance.

"What do you think?" Lotti asked at his side, sounding nervous.

He turned to her and shook his head with a low laugh. "I think it's perfect."

Her smile was warm and relieved, and the vise that had been around his heart since this morning when he'd realized the craziest thing—that he was falling for her all over again—tightened.

The roads were being cleared even as they stood here. Estimated time of opening was tomorrow morning. This meant that at best he had twenty-four hours to make her start to fall too.

"It all looks good," she said. "You pulled it off."

"*We* pulled it off."

She turned to him, her smile fading, but before she could speak, Finn came up the makeshift aisle. He was in dress pants and a slate gray button down—the same that he'd worn to the bachelor/bachelorette party. Looking uncharacteristically nervous, he fussed with his tie until it was crooked.

"Here," Sean said and knocked his brother's hands away. "I've got it. What the hell's wrong with you?" he asked when he realized Finn was sweating. "You wanted this."

"Still do," Finn said. "More than I want anything else in the entire world." His serious gaze met Sean's. "This is the most important thing I'll ever do."

And *that* was why he was nervous, Sean realized. "Hey man, you got this. And I've got you. So no worries."

Finn let out a long, shaky exhale and nodded. "Thanks."

Sean turned to Lotti and found her studying him with a look he'd never seen before, like maybe she was proud of him. He had to admit, he didn't hate that.

"And shouldn't you be the anxious one?" Finn asked Sean. "You're the guy who has to marry us. All I've gotta do is say 'I do.'"

"True," Sean said.

"I mean it's you who has to make sure it all happens here today," Finn went on. "That nothing goes wrong, that it's absolutely perfect. So . . . are you? Nervous?"

Well he was now. "How hard can it be?" he asked with what he hoped was a calm voice. No need to share with the class that he was shaking in his boots. "Take this ring, I thee wed, cherish and obey, yadda yadda, right?" he asked.

Finn laughed. "Dude, if you put 'obey' in the vows, Pru's going to kill you where you stand."

"Oh, I had it for *your* part of the vows, not hers."

Finn grabbed him in a headlock and they tussled for a minute, like old times.

And then, less than a half an hour later, Archer was walking Pru down the aisle toward Finn. Seeing the love shining so brilliantly between the two of them after saying "with the power invested in me by GetOrdained.com, Finn, kiss your bride!" Watching as they laughed and Pru jumped into Finn's arms while everyone hugged. Sean knew he'd never forget a minute of this trip.

Lotti came up to his side and he looked at her. Huh. She *was* proud of him. "You were amazing," she said.

He didn't quite feel amazing. He felt . . . something he couldn't quite define. Not that there was time to think because they all moved back the furniture, kicked up the music, danced, drank, and ate.

And then danced, drank, and ate some more.

Watching, feeling oddly enough a little bit like he was on the outside looking in, Sean realized what was wrong.

He was *lonely*, even while surrounded by the people who meant the most to him in the world. How that could be the case, he honestly had no idea. He picked up the bottle of Corona in front of him and took a long pull. It'd been years since he'd been intoxicated, but tonight was definitely the end of a long dry spell. He smiled as Finn and Pru made their way around the makeshift dance floor. He'd never seen Finn so happy.

Never.

They made a great couple, appreciating and recognizing what they had, what they'd worked so hard for. It was their night and no one deserved it more.

Sean's eyes searched out Lotti for the thousandth time. She wore a midnight colored dress, short and molded perfectly to her soft curves and showing off some gorgeous legs that he wanted wrapped around him. She'd started out the evening with her hair carefully twisted at the back of her head. Some of it had escaped. Tendrils framed her flushed face and fell over her bare shoulders and back, teasing her skin.

She was so beautiful she made his chest hurt. But ever since the ceremony, during which she had adorably teared up, she'd been different. Holding herself back.

The rancher from next door had showed up a

few minutes ago with another case of beer that
he'd found in his back refrigerator. Lotti was talking to him, thanking him, a soft smile playing at
the corners of her mouth.

It didn't matter how many times Sean saw her
smile, he still felt the pleasure from it like it was
the first time, back at that football game . . . He'd
had no right to touch her that night, but he had.

He had even less right to touch her now. He'd
had his chance and he'd walked away from her.

Man, he'd been such a stupid sixteen-year-old
punk.

But God, he hoped like hell that second chances
were really a thing as he finished off his beer and
made his way over to her. This wasn't going to be
on the top ten list of the smartest things he'd ever
done, but at that moment he didn't care.

Archer stepped into his path. "Whatcha doing?"

"Nothing," Sean said.

"Nothing, or you're about to go interrupt a really great woman from getting a dance invite?"

Sean met Archer's gaze and Archer went brows
up. "We're leaving here soon enough," Archer said.

Like Sean didn't know. "And?"

"And . . . don't needlessly complicate things for
her."

Sean looked over at Lotti, who was smiling up
into the rancher's face. "Archer?"

"Yeah?"

"Remember when you *needlessly* complicated
Elle's life?"

Archer sighed.

"Just tell me this—what would you have done if I'd tried to stop you?" Sean asked.

Archer conceded gracefully. "Probably taken out a few of your front teeth." He backed up a step, hands in the air, signaling that Sean should carry on as he planned.

So Sean once again headed toward Lotti. He'd made his life about freedom and no complications. But he'd been fighting a restlessness, an aching loneliness for a while now. He hadn't known what to do about it, but he knew now.

He walked up to Lotti and the rancher just in time to hear the guy ask her to dance. "Can I cut in?" Sean asked, not that he was going to take no for an answer.

The rancher's gaze slid first to Lotti, who was still just staring up at Sean, before nodding curtly and stepping away from her.

Sean took Lotti's hand and brought her to the dance floor. Her eyes were guarded and she felt a little stiff in his arms as he pulled her in close for the slow song.

"You had all night to ask me to dance," she said. "Why did you pick that very moment?"

"Why are you already distancing yourself from me?" he asked instead of responding to the question for which he didn't have any good answer to give. "I haven't even left yet."

"But you're going to," she said.

Yeah. She had him there. He pulled her in close,

drinking in her familiar scent, molding his body to
hers so that he felt the exact second she melted into
him. When she sighed, he knew he wasn't alone
in this, no matter what she wanted him to believe.
They had something, something deep and meaningful and everlasting. Running a hand down the
length of her back, he closed his eyes to savor the
feel of her bare skin beneath his fingers.

"Sean?"

He opened his eyes and realized every gaze in
the room was on them. He slid them all a hard look
that said *mind your own fucking business for once* and
led Lotti over to a more secluded part of the room,
on the other side of the huge Christmas tree, where
he could continue to hold on to her without their
avid audience.

"So about the distance thing," he said.

"We're not going there," she said. "You're leaving. The end."

He looked into her eyes. "Are you saying you
have no interest in letting me be a part of your
life?"

"But see, that's just it. You're *not* a part of my
life," she said. "You're a fantasy. One that's about
to go poof and vanish."

"It doesn't have to be like that, Lotti."

She gave him a get real look. "Yeah. I've heard
that before."

Okay, he deserved her disbelief and probably a
lot more. But he knew this wasn't about him, or
even her feelings for him. "You've got cold feet

again," he said. "And no one would blame you for that, Lotti. No one. But—"

"I've always rushed too fast," she said. "Rushed to my happily ever after, and it's never worked out for me."

"It only takes one," he said.

She stared at him like he'd lost his mind. "Stop doing this."

"Stop doing what? Wanting you? Wanting you to want me?"

"It was just a weekend."

He looked into her eyes and saw old hurts and new fears. Fears that he might hurt her . . . again. Legitimate. He leaned in and touched his mouth to the shell of her ear. "It feels like a lot more than a weekend," he confessed.

She didn't say anything to this but she did settle in against him eventually relaxing in his arms. After that he let the beat of the music carry them. He felt ridiculous when he started to dread the end of the song. He didn't want to lose the physical contact, and as if maybe she felt the same, her hands tightened around his neck and she pressed her face into his throat.

"I'm sorry, Lotti," he said. "So damned sorry for what I did to you."

"No, I was messed up, thinking that my first lover was The One. No sixteen-year-old boy could've lived up to my expectations. Hell, even now, no one could. In fact . . ." She shook her head. "I make sure they can't. My fiancé . . ."

"I know," he said. "He was an ass too. Leaving you a week before your wedding—"

"It was my fault, Sean."

"No. No way."

"Yes way," she said. She grimaced and shook her head. "I kept changing the date of the wedding, pushing it back. It was my way of sabotaging. It's what I do, I push people away. And I'm good at it, Sean." She stepped back, and he could see in her eyes it was more than the song ending.

They were ending before they'd even gotten started. "Wait," he said. "What happened to eating the cookies, to reading books for pleasure, to singing in the rain and jumping into the puddles?" He paused until she met his gaze. "What happened to falling in love with a blast from your past?"

"I . . . I never said that last part. Sean—"

He could see in her eyes what she was about to say. "Lotti, don't—"

"I promised myself I'd start learning from the mistakes of my past instead of repeating them." And then she stepped out of his arms and walked away.

Just as he'd once done to her.

THE next morning dawned gray and dark, but nothing was falling out of the sky at least. Sean reached for his phone and checked the weather and roads.

The worst of the storm had passed. The roads

were a mess, many still impassable but they were starting to slowly let people through. They could get out.

And sure enough, an hour later, Sean stood watching as his friends loaded up the van. He had his bag packed, but he wasn't ready to leave.

He wasn't ever going to be ready to leave.

Determined to tell Lotti that very thing, he turned to go find her—but she was right there, a nervous smile curving her mouth. "Can I talk to you for a sec?" she asked.

"You can talk to me for as long as you want." *Forever,* he thought. *Talk to me forever so I don't have to leave.*

She swallowed hard and looked down at her clipboard. "Well, I've been thinking."

"Which explains the smoke coming out of your ears."

She let out a low laugh. "Yeah. I do tend to over-think things. I like to obsess over every decision until it's nearly impossible to make. Which is why I'm changing things up." She met his gaze. "I over-thought this weekend."

Unable to help himself, he closed the distance between them and cupped her jaw. "There's nothing to overthink. What we shared here was a second chance, and I don't intend to let it pass us by." He leaned in and kissed her. "I want to see you again, Lotti. As soon as you'll let me. I'm going to call. Text. Email. FaceTime. Whatever it takes to show you I'm serious. We're only forty minutes away from each other. That's nothing. *Nothing*," he repeated, setting a finger over her lips when she opened her mouth. "And I know you have no reason at all to believe me, to believe *in* me, but it's okay. All I need is some time to show you."

She took a gentle nip out of his finger. "I want to see you again too."

His heart leapt. "Yeah?"

"Yeah and . . . well, I sort of have a confession." She pulled a piece of paper from her clipboard. Her Cabo itinerary. "I thought we could rebook my flights," she said. "And add a plus one because I was hoping you'd come with. I mean, I know your brother just got married so you're undoubtedly in charge of the pub when you get back, so we can time it so that it works out for everyone. If you're interested . . ."

He had to pause because the emotion and relief and hope that flooded him took away his ability to speak for a second.

"I mean, I know it's a big deal to go on vacay together when we hardly know each other, but it doesn't have to be any sort of pressure or anything," she said softly, letting him see the emotion and hope in her eyes. But there were nerves too. She was worried he'd say no.

"Yes," he said.

"Yes, you're okay with no pressure or yes to—"

"Yes to all of it," he said. "Everything. Whatever you want." And then he sealed the vow with a kiss.

Epilogue

Cᴀʙᴏ ᴡᴀꜱ everything Napa hadn't been. Warm, sunny . . . *perfect,* Lotti thought on a dreamy sigh. Sean had upgraded their accommodations to a villa with a private pool and its own access to the beach. He said he'd done it because he wanted to go skinny-dipping with her, but she knew there was another reason as well.

He didn't want anything to remind her of the honeymoon this trip had been planned for, showing another surprising side to Sean O'Riley. A sweet side.

There were other ways in which he'd made sure that this trip didn't remind her of anything in her past. Of course, most of those ways had occurred in bed. And on the kitchenette counter. And the patio lounger. And the shower . . .

At the moment, she was on the lounger sunning while Sean was on the phone, checking in at home. She flopped over on her stomach and untied the back of her bikini so she wouldn't get a tan line. The air was warm and salty and she could hear the waves, which lulled her into dozing off.

She woke up as two big, slightly callused hands ran up and down her body and smiled. "Mmm, Thor," she murmured. "Don't stop."

A low, masculine growl had her smiling. "Don't worry," she murmured. "My boyfriend's on the phone. We've got plenty of time."

She squeaked when she was lifted in the air and tossed over Sean's shoulder like a sack of potatoes and carried toward the pool.

"Oh no," she said, laughing. "I can't get my hair wet before we go out to dinner."

He didn't slow down.

"Sean! I'm not kidding! You're closing in on batshit crazy if you think I've time to fix this mop before those fancy reservations you made—"

He was still moving and all she could see was the smooth, sinewy expanse of his tanned back and those low-riding board shorts emphasizing his great ass. "Stop!" She was laughing so hard she could scarcely talk. "Sean, wait! I take it back! You're not closing in on batshit crazy . . ."

He paused in his progress and slid a hand to her ass. "No?"

"No," she said. "I'd never imply that you'd do anything halfway." She paused. "You're *completely* batshit crazy."

His shoulders were shaking with laughter as he put her down on the top step inside the pool. The water was a perfect seventy-eight degrees so she felt no twinge of guilt when she smiled up at him sweetly, sexily, making a promise with her eyes, causing him to smile at her in return as she . . .

Shoved him backward into the pool.

It would've been the perfect move if he hadn't been as fast as a cat, a big, bad mountain cat who snagged her around the ankle and took her in with him.

She laughed at the shock of the water and was still laughing when he kissed her. It was one of those kisses that started off sweet but then escalated quickly. Her bikini top was floating away on the water before she could blink and Sean slid his tongue over a taut nipple, making goose bumps race along her skin.

"Give me a chance," he said against her lips.

She pulled back to meet his gaze, having to blink a couple of times before the words he'd spoken could sink in. "What?"

He cupped her face in the palm of his hand. His thumb stroked over her cheekbone as he studied her eyes. "I want you to give me a chance."

"A chance at what?"

Shifting so that he could press his forehead to hers, he said one word. "You."

Her breath caught. "Sean," she breathed.

"Because you've got me," he said. "All of me. I'm falling in love you, Lotti, heart and soul. I know it's too soon for you. I know you're scared. I know you're not sure about me. I know it's going to take time, but I've got that to give and more. I can wait. You're worth it."

She couldn't tear her gaze off him, this incredible, amazing man who'd had her heart from all those years ago. "We must both be crazy."

"Because . . . ?"

"Because I'm falling for you too, Sean." There were other words that needed to be said. A lot. They'd have to talk more, but she had that one thing of his that she had begun to crave. His heart. And for now that was enough.

MISTLETOE IN PARADISE

Prologue

Christmas, twelve years ago

Fourteen-year-old Hannah Banfield stood at the very edge of a cliff. Not a mental cliff, which would have been less terrifying. Nope, she was stupid enough to be standing on an actual rocky bluff, toes hanging off as she stared down at the Caribbean blue-green sea swirling *hundreds* of thousands of feet below her.

"Twenty," came the amused male voice at her side. "It's twenty feet."

She slid her gaze to James Webber, ancient and full of wisdom at age fifteen. "We're going to die."

Tall, gangly, his messy dark brown hair weeks past needing a cut, he flashed her his crooked smile. His board shorts hung nearly to his knees, one of which was scraped and bleeding from when she'd accidentally tripped him on the hike up here. "We're not going to die," he said.

"How do you know?"

"Because I won't let it happen."

She closed her eyes and drew in a deep breath

at his low but firm tone of confidence, letting it fill her. When the humid, salty sea breeze warmed her, she opened her eyes and stalled by looking around her at the small private island where their families always spent at least one day of their Christmas getaway. She took in the bright white sand, palm trees, and lush green bluffs, all of which were just about as far away from her snowy mountain view at home in the California Sierras as she could get.

James nudged her. "You know how I know we're going to live? Because Jason did. Look."

They both eyed James's brother in the water below, waving wildly up at them. A year older than James, Jason was their fearless leader, and as such, he'd jumped first.

Their moms were BFFs. The women had grown up together, but as adults now lived on opposite coasts in the United States. Since Hannah's stepdad, Harry, was a year-round captain of a charter yacht, the two families booked the ship before Christmas every year to be together. They had what was called a bareboat charter, meaning they did all the work of the crew to make it affordable, not that any of them had ever minded. Well, except maybe her mom, who didn't like to cook and clean off the boat, much less on it.

For James and Jason, the annual trip was a chance to get away from the cold New York winters. But for Hannah, it was so much more. The weeklong cruise from Miami to St. Thomas and back was a place where she could be a kid, since her life in Real World was very different from that in Vacation World. For this one week she got to be . . . well, free. Happy. Plus, she considered the Webber brothers her two closest friends, trusting them more than anyone else.

"You've got this, Hannah Banana," James said softly.

He might be the wildest, most adventurous person she knew, but he'd never put her in danger. So she drew a deep breath and stared down at the water one last time. She wanted to do this, wanted so much to show that she could be spontaneous and fun too, though she wasn't. Were there sharks in the Caribbean Sea? There were, right? She swallowed hard. "I don't think I can," she whispered.

"Hey. Hey, it's okay." His bigger, warmer hand slid into hers and squeezed. "But you know I've got you, though, right?"

She looked into his warm blue-green eyes, the same color as the sea below, and just like that, she believed. He *always* had her. Maybe all of the other people in her life had let her down, but never him. Not once.

So she gave a slow nod.

Smart enough not to give her another second to think about it, he simply jumped, tugging her with him into the balmy Caribbean air.

Chapter One

Four days before Christmas, present day

HANNAH STOOD on a dock in Miami in front of the ship aptly named *The Therapist*. The seventy-foot motor yacht, a good decade past its prime, was decorated for the holidays within an inch of its life. Staring at it with dread, she wished she hadn't chosen this month to cut back on wine. Because she'd taken two planes, a train, and an automobile to get here, and worrying about blood pressure and heart disease was taking a backseat to what she was going to face on the ship.

Unfortunately, she was on a mission, and sucky as that mission was, she owed it to the man who'd raised her to do this in person, even if her palms were sweating.

And the backs of her knees.

The mission—tell her stepdad, Harry, that her mom wanted a divorce, and by the way, the papers were right here in her bag for him to sign. Oh, and Merry Christmas.

Easy peasy.

Except she loved Harry. He was the only dad she'd ever known. He'd brought fun and adventure and humor into her life when there'd been so little before him. She loved his slightly run-down but beloved yacht, the one she'd spent every Christmas on for as long as she could remember to escape winter by sailing through the Caribbean.

At least until six years ago.

"Ahoy, Smalls!" came Harry's booming voice from the boat deck. He stood there in Bermuda shorts, a brightly flowered short-sleeved shirt, and a Santa hat on his Albert Einstein hair, looking like . . . home. "Come aboard," he called out, "this baby ain't going to sail herself."

Knowing the truth of that, Hannah laughed, then opened her purse and pulled out a big red bow, setting it on top of her head as proof she'd come through on her word that this year, her holiday gift to him was her presence on *The Therapist*.

She headed up the passerelle, the platform from dock to ship, which in itself felt odd. For all the years she'd come here, she'd never once *walked* onboard. Nope, she'd flat-out run, racing to pick out her cabin in order to get the one she wanted—the one with the porthole—before it was snatched up by James and Jason.

But that was then. Things had changed.

In a big way.

At the end of the passerelle, she kicked off her boots and dropped them into the waiting shoe basket. As was traditional on boats like this, shoes weren't allowed, and as she stood there in her bare feet, taking it all in, a pit grew in the bottom of her stomach. It'd been this very boat that had eventually caused the split between Harry and her mom, almost ten years ago now. Harry had been gone almost all the time on charters, and finally her mom had said, "It's me or the boat." Harry had chosen the boat.

By the time he'd realized his mistake, her mom had moved on.

Hannah had worked hard to not judge Harry for picking the boat over his family. Her mom was a difficult woman. Hannah got that. Well, mostly she got that.

Seen from the perspective of Hannah's adult eyes, *The Therapist* was a little rough around the edges now, but was still pretty amazing, with its five-foot cockpit extension, huge teak-top deck half-covered and half-open to the warm Caribbean air, large galley, and four cabins besides the captain's chambers.

She dropped her duffel bag just as Harry pulled her in for a big, warm hug. She sighed out some of her tension and held on tight as memories filled her—his teaching her to drive a boat before she could even ride a bike; his showing her fun and adventure for a week every Christmas, joy that'd had to last her the whole year . . .

Harry pulled back and grinned at her. "You're the best Christmas present I've ever had. It's been too long. The last time I saw you was this spring, when

I was off for a week and we went fishing." He looked past her to the busy port. "Where's your mom?"

Hannah blinked. "Um . . . what?"

"You know, the woman who birthed you? She said she was coming this year and traveling with you."

Thanks, Mom. "She . . ." Suddenly Hannah's purse, the one that held the divorce papers for Harry, weighed heavily on her shoulder. "So as it turns out, she's—"

"Hold on. I just got a text from her. She's going to meet us in the port of San Juan on our Puerto Rico stop, and then be with us on the last leg to St. Thomas and back home," Harry said, reading from his phone. "She got held up at work."

Hannah's mouth tightened at the lie. Her mom's, not Harry's. Since the separation, her mom had still occasionally joined them—in between boyfriends, that is—just enough times to keep Harry's hopes up. But now her mom wanted to marry her latest boyfriend. She'd told Harry she'd come on this trip, but she'd lost her nerve and had planned to pay a courier to do her dirty work.

Hannah couldn't let a stranger serve Harry the papers, she just couldn't. So here she was, facing more than a few ghosts of her own past as well as her mom's.

Harry was smiling warmly at her. "I'm so glad you showed up."

She forced a smile. "When have I ever broken a promise or let you down?"

Guilt flashed across his craggy, been-in-the-sun-for-fifty-plus-years face because he knew he couldn't say the same. "You're as sweet as you are dependable."

Right, just what every woman wanted to hear, a description of herself employing the same adjectives as those applied to a golden retriever.

Harry pulled off his hat and dropped his phone into it. "No more of this on vacay. All it does is bring bad news." He held out the hat. Guess he could hear her phone, which had been buzzing since she'd boarded. Work, no doubt. She could tell by the sheer level of annoyance in the vibration. Pulling it from her pocket, she eyed the screen. Yep. Her boss, Cynthia, aka the Tyrant, as the office often called her. Cynthia thought it was a compliment.

"Come on now, Smalls," Harry said. "Drop that evil ruination of modern society into the hat. You're my gift this year, and I don't plan on sharing you with your job 24/7 like usual."

"Okay, but, Dad, remember, I did warn you that I'd have to work some. That was the only reason I got the time away from the office for this trip."

Harry didn't say anything to this. Instead, he turned to the woman who'd just come from the bridge to stand at his side. Sally, his longtime stewardess and self-appointed cruise director, handed Hannah what looked like a frothy eggnog and a festive elf headpiece, complete with a little green hat.

Sally laughed at the look on Hannah's face. "I

know. But Harry insisted. All passengers-slash-coworkers have to be in the proper festive spirit this week."

The thing about boating with Harry this week was that he didn't make money, so he gave his crew the time off, which meant it was all hands on deck. "Just how many others are we talking about?"

"Well, Susan and Dan, of course," Harry said, referring to the Webbers. "And you and your mom, and—"

Hannah's phone rang again.

"Nope," Harry said and jiggled his hat. He always collected cell phones at the start of a trip, mostly because Harry had never met a responsibility he couldn't put away, not to be seen until it suited him.

"Dad—"

"Nope. And I'm doing you a favor, trust me."

She grimaced in apology but answered the phone. "Hannah Banfield."

Harry rolled his eyes.

"So you do live," Cynthia said in her no-nonsense, perpetually irritated voice. "Is there a reason you're not checking your damn phone in the middle of a very important week when you've got a very big case being decided upon?"

Three years ago, the woman had taken a chance on Hannah, teaching her the ropes when Hannah had started with no specific experience, only her painful ambition. Hannah was now a successful health care advocate, working for the hospital in her hometown and fighting on behalf of insurance rights for terminal patients. She was incredibly proud of the work she was doing. But because she'd made the mistake of asking her dad what he wanted for Christmas, and because his answer had been only one thing—*her*—she was here, and Cynthia was going to get heartburn *and* the chance to take Hannah's case in front of a judge. "I'm sorry," she said. "What's up?"

"I've emailed you several files. I've marked my questions. The last thing we want is the judge to postpone until after the holidays."

"I'll take a look," Hannah promised and disconnected.

Her dad wriggled the hat for her cell phone. "This is vacation."

"Come on, Dad, I'm turning twenty-seven years, not twelve. And who's the other guest?"

Harry just smiled, giving her a very bad feeling. But it couldn't be. Her mom had told her James was in Belize with a girlfriend, which suited her just fine.

Totally, one hundred percent fine.

Fine.

His parents were no problem, she loved them. But when it came to James, her feelings were . . . complicated. That's when she realized Harry was smiling at someone just behind her, and then a long arm reached around her to drop a phone into the Santa hat.

Slowly she swiveled and came face-to-face with a blast from the past. The kind of blast that stole her breath away and rendered her stock-still. The kind of blast that was sexy and familiar at the same time, and brought both the best and the worst memories of her life slamming back into her.

James Webber, who was clearly *not* in Belize.

Her dad grinned at him. "Hey, WK! Good to see you, kid."

WK was short for Wild Kid, and there'd been plenty of years when James had merited the nickname. He was a grown man now, but Harry still saw both of them as kids.

Not looking bothered by the handle at all, James exchanged a warm, back-slapping hug with Harry. Then he looked at Hannah, and the result was good news and bad news. The good news—she managed to keep her cool and give him an "I'm totally okay that you're here" smile. The bad news—his crooked smile was still a killer, and those warm blue-green eyes still promised fun and trouble that she *knew* he could deliver on. Suddenly needing that hopefully strong eggnog, she took a healthy swallow, then promptly began to choke up a lung.

James patted her on the back until she waved him away and glared at her father. *"Virgin?"*

"I *always* serve you virgin."

"Yeah, when I was a kid."

"You're still a kid." He spread his arms. "Because I'm only twenty-nine."

"You've been twenty-nine for twenty-nine years."

"Hey, knock that off. Reality doesn't have a role here in Vacay Land."

James accepted a glass from Sally. He drank, and then his eyes were flat-out laughing.

Clearly *not* virgin.

"Wow," she said to her dad, looking away from James, because it'd been a huge mistake to look directly at him. How was it that he looked even better now than he had back then?

Especially because back then he'd been naked.

At the memory of the last time she'd seen him, she reached over the bar against the back of the deck, grabbed the bottle of dark rum, and poured it into her glass.

James looked amused.

"You should both go get settled before I put you to work," Harry said. "There's a storm brewing, so as soon as Dan and Susan arrive, we need to get ahead of it." He nodded at Sally to follow him to the bridge.

When they were gone, Hannah let out a slow breath. Great. A storm on the horizon, and another in her stomach. She took another sip of her eggnog, knowing it was going to help when it burned all the way down.

James stood there, eyes amused. She couldn't stop herself from looking right back. Barefoot, he was wearing jeans that fit him in all the right spots, an untucked thin army-green T-shirt tight across his chest and loose across his abs. Damn. Why did he still appeal to her? Not that it mattered—he was most definitely *not* on the menu for the week.

Been there, been destroyed by it.

"Hannah Banana in the flesh," he said. "Been a while."

She added another dollop of rum, and he laughed softly.

She took a big gulp before meeting that gaze of his, the one that tended to make her stupid. "Thought you were going to be in Belize with your girlfriend. Hope you didn't get dumped."

He smiled. "The trip got moved up. I got back last week, but Candy and I had a great time, so thanks for your concern."

She refrained from rolling her eyes. Probably Candy was a perfectly nice person. She wasn't annoyed by Candy. She was annoyed by the man standing there looking better than anything she'd seen in a long time.

James picked up the duffel bag he'd dropped at his feet. "And while you finish up that drink that you look like you really need, I'm going to grab the good cabin."

Oh hell no.

Their eyes caught and held, and then they each took off running at the same time, and for a moment it was like they were kids again.

Until James stopped short and pointed starboard. "Hey, what's that?"

Like a sucker, she skidded to a halt and looked.

Nothing.

And James was running again.

"Cheater!" she yelled, running after him.

He just laughed, moving with the easy grace of a lifelong athlete.

Something no one had *ever* accused her of being.

Pushing herself to catch up, she accidentally—sort of—knocked him into a wall. Still laughing, he snagged her arm, yanking her behind him, and kept the lead.

So she pulled out the big guns and fought dirty. She hit the floor with a soft, pained gasp.

"Oh shit," he said. Whipping back around, he dropped to his knees at her side. "What is it? Your ankle?"

"Nope!" She was on her feet and running, laughing so hard she couldn't breathe. She had this! She was going to get the cabin with the porthole. Already grinning in triumph, just before she got to the door, she turned and sent him a smug smile over her shoulder.

Which was when he snatched her around the waist and manhandled her aside to get to the door first.

But the deal was that it was the first person to the bed. So she took a flying leap and hit him in the back, and . . . they both landed on the bunk at the same time.

They were laughing and grappling as they bounced, and suddenly she realized James was flat on his back sprawled with limbs akimbo, and she was on top of him, pinning him down. "Um . . ."

She went still and stared at him, heart pounding, head spinning.

As for what *he* was feeling . . . she had zero idea. He was much better at hiding his emotions, but she sure as hell hoped he was feeling tortured by his feelings.

"Nice hat," he said.

"Dammit." She tugged the elf headpiece off. The bow too.

He hadn't moved, just continued to stare up at her, the air seeming to crackle around them, and not from the incoming storm. Needing to cut the sudden tension, Hannah scrambled off him, sitting back on her heels on the foot of the bed. "You'll still do anything to win, I see," she turned to quip.

He sat up as well, smile long gone. "Good thing, then, that this time all I'm interested in winning is some peace and quiet." Pushing off the bed, he headed to the door.

"You're leaving?" she asked his back. "You're letting me have this cabin without a fight?"

"We're not kids anymore, Hannah." His mouth quirked very slightly, but he didn't smile. "And I'm not doing this with you again. Once was enough for me." He paused. "Though I'll admit watching you hitch up that sundress to race me is going to stick with me for many nights to come."

She looked down at her sundress, mostly as a delay tactic, because he was right, of course. What had happened was all on her. "Look," she said in a low voice, "I just need to give something to Harry, and then I'll leave, and you and your parents can have the whole week to yourselves, okay?"

He looked surprised. "Okay."

So he wasn't going to try to keep her here. Fair, though also hurtful. She scooted off the bed and then nearly hit the floor when the boat rocked.

They stared at each other in shock.

"Are we—" She shook her head. "No. He wouldn't. It's probably just the tide coming in."

"It's too early for the tide." He moved to the porthole. "Shit."

She rushed to the porthole too, elbow to elbow with him. "Oh my god."

"Yeah," he said grimly. "We've set sail."

Chapter Two

BOTH JAMES and Hannah hit the door running, racing back in the direction they'd just come, down the narrow hallway and up the stairs. James had no idea what her thoughts were, but his were *hell no*. No way was he going to get stuck on this boat with Hannah Banfield. No way, no how.

He'd been thrown off-balance when he'd first boarded and seen her standing there with Harry, as if the past six years hadn't happened.

Like maybe Jason was still alive . . .

Just his brain messing with him again, of course. Because Jason was long gone.

James was no longer drowning in grief. He had his head above water. He was finally, *finally* starting to get used to his new normal, living in a world with his two best friends gone. One dead. One—Hannah—gone by choice.

And yet here she was, all five feet seven inches of sexy curves and curly honey-brown hair flying around her face, with milk chocolate eyes he'd happily drowned in more than once—a fact he was doing his best to forget. Above deck, he looked around, stunned to find Miami's shoreline was already far away, and stopped short.

Hannah plowed into the back of him, and he reached back to steady her. When she held her own, he turned to her, the woman he was stuck at sea with, the first woman he'd ever fallen for. And while logically he knew he was long over it, over her, there was nothing rational about how just looking at her had made his heart roll over in his chest and expose its underbelly.

She gave him a look he couldn't begin to interpret and then stalked to the cockpit.

Harry stood there, hands on the helm as he steered, chewing on an unlit cigar, looking fully at ease as he eyed the navigation systems.

"What the actual hell, Dad?" Hannah asked.

Harry glanced over at them. "Problem?"

"Are you kidding me?"

Harry flashed his stepdaughter a grin before looking at James. "Just got a text from your parents. They never got out of New York. Planes are grounded due to a massive snowstorm. They're going to catch up with us in San Juan."

A stay of execution . . .

"Take us back, Dad," Hannah said.

"No can do, Smalls. We've got our own storm system moving in. No worries, though. If all goes to plan, we'll stay well ahead of it."

"Dad, this is silly. There's no reason for you to waste the fuel and rations for only the two of us. Just take us back."

At the emotion in her voice, Harry took his gaze off the horizon to look at her.

James did not. He'd already soaked up the sight of her in that adorably sexy sundress. Plus, he'd just quite literally been beneath her, which had stirred up a lot of things best forgotten. His brain knew this, it did. But the rest of him hadn't quite caught up. He hadn't seen her in years, and the last time he had was right here on this boat, when he'd watched her walk away from him.

"This isn't happening," she said, tossing up her hands. "Turn us around."

"As I mentioned, James's parents are going to catch up with us in Puerto Rico. Same with your mom, I'm sure." He smiled around the cigar. "Damn, it's going to be great to all be together again."

"Dad, that's at least three days from now."

Harry looked over the instruments, did a quick calculation, and shook his head. "Actually, with the headwind, maybe even four."

"Look, Dad . . . just don't get your heart set on this, okay? You know how Mom can be."

"No, this year she's coming," Harry said firmly. "I can feel it."

Hannah didn't say anything to this, just slid dark sunglasses on her face. But the worry wasn't hard to read, concern likely with good reason. Leslie Banfield liked to make promises, but she wasn't as fond of keeping them. Same as Harry. Growing up, James had hated that for Hannah.

She had her arms crossed over her chest. Clearly there was something more than just worry on her mind.

James knew this woman. Or at least he'd known the girl she'd once been. She was smart as hell, passionate, and incredibly dedicated to those she cared about.

Once upon a time he'd been one of those people.

"Dad, this isn't funny," Hannah said.

And yeah, there was definitely something more in her voice besides worry. He turned to her. "What's going on?"

She kept her gaze on her dad. "You mean other than the captain kidnapping us against our will?"

Harry sighed. "Do you really want to be the one to call your mom and tell her we're not spending Christmas together this year?"

"Dad—"

"See this little dot?" Harry asked, pointing to his screen. "That's us. See this other dot over there? That's the port of San Juan. That's how far we have to go. So nothing personal, Smalls, but I'd rather take on you two any day of the week than a pissed-off Leslie."

Guilt. That was the unnamed emotion on Hannah's face, and it flashed again now. Not that James gave a shit. All he did give a damn about was the fact that for at least three days, maybe four, they were stuck on this boat together—a complete nightmare. Especially since he still had absolutely no idea what had happened the last time he and Hannah had been together.

Granted, he'd been royally messed up at that time. Years ago, Jason had died of a rare and misdiagnosed heart condition. His family had fallen apart, and James had . . . lost himself. So much so that he'd asked Hannah to walk away from her life and go explore the planet with him. She'd declined and ghosted him. Probably she'd been the smart one. He'd spent the next year doing the wanderlust thing in between helping his dad run the family lumber business. Eventually he had become an expedition guide, which had mended his heart. Somewhat. The last he'd heard about Hannah, she'd been dating some suit.

He could insist on going back. He'd known Harry for most of his life. He was a lot of things, and reasonable wasn't always one of them, but at heart he was a good guy. He wouldn't keep James here against his will.

But looking at Harry and Hannah staring at each other now, both wary and hurting and unsure of their footing together, he knew he wouldn't be the one to make them turn around. They needed these days together—anyone who cared about either of them could see that.

And like it or not, James did care about them. More than he wanted to admit. But that didn't mean he wanted to be a part of it, so he turned and walked away, his goal being to lie low and try to stay out of the way of any emotional turmoil. He had his own problems coming his way as soon as his dad met up with them in Puerto Rico. Plus— and this was the biggie—he'd had enough emotional turmoil to last him a lifetime.

Chapter Three

LATE THAT night, they set anchor near the Bahamas. Hannah had spent the day helping Sally. They fixed dinner and prepped the next day's meals, and then had gone through the daily maintenance routine.

She was aware that James was assisting her dad, but their paths didn't cross—which on a seventy-foot boat was a miracle, or she wasn't the only one using avoidance techniques.

Well done.

She waited until her dad had consumed his usual bedtime cocktail and passed out before sneaking into his quarters to steal back her phone. It wasn't hard to see in the cabin because he had twinkle lights hung across the room, blinking in festive red and green. Through the holiday glow, she easily spotted her phone on his dresser, along with another. She tiptoed into the room, but she could've been a bull in a china shop and he wouldn't have been able to hear her over his own snoring.

She eyed the two phones, flashing back to James dropping his phone into the Santa hat without argument. She knew from her mom that he helped out with the family lumber business but also ran his own expedition company. Surely he needed his phone too, right? After all, what if *Candy* wanted to reach him? Or *sext* him?

With a sigh, she grabbed both phones and was backing out of the room when from the corner of her eye she caught sight of a shadow watching her and nearly screamed.

James.

She opened her mouth, but he put a finger against her lips and pulled her into the hallway, carefully and quietly shutting her dad's door.

"Hannah Banana, sexy cat burglar," he murmured. "Who knew?"

"I needed my phone. I've got work to do."

"Of course you do."

She opened her mouth to further explain, but he shook his head. "None of my business," he said.

Right. And true, but a little part of her felt . . . sad? There'd been a time when they'd known everything about each other. Now the only thing she knew for sure was that he'd hoped to make this trip without her. She was silently grappling with that when one of the two phones in her pocket buzzed with an unfamiliar tone. Pulling it from her pocket, she tossed it to James. "When you scared me half to death, I forgot I also liberated your phone for you."

He simply slid it into his pocket. Still ringing. She stared at him. He'd changed into cargo shorts, but still wore the same T-shirt. As per yachting rules to protect the teak flooring, he was still barefoot, as was she. There was something about being barefoot with someone that felt . . . oddly intimate. "You're not even going to look and see who was calling?" she asked in shocked disbelief. "It could be important. Maybe it's Candy."

"I'm off-line. And she wouldn't be calling me."

Okay, that actually told her nothing. "But . . ." This was unfathomable to her. "What if it's work?"

"I'm unreachable to work. It's called a vacation, Hannah. Everyone should unplug once in a while. Especially people like you."

She narrowed her eyes. "People like me?"

"People who can't unplug from work because they don't have a life."

She gaped at him. "I have a life."

"Good."

"I *do*!"

"I said *good*."

She eyed his pocket, which was lit up from his phone inside it. "What about the people who might need to get ahold of you who *aren't* your work?"

"The people who matter most to me either know where I am or are here."

She sucked in a breath, having no idea what to do with that, plus still stinging from the "people like you" comment.

"Have you talked to your dad yet?" he asked.

Startled, she blinked. "What?"

"I could tell earlier that you were holding something back from him. Figured you were here to talk to him about something."

Nice to know she was still transparent. "It's nothing that concerns you."

He looked at her for a long beat, then nodded, and with one last unreadable look, he vanished down the dark hallway.

THE next morning, Hannah awoke at the crack of dawn. Actually, that statement wasn't quite accurate. In order to wake up, she would have had to have gotten some sleep—which she hadn't. She lay there registering the gentle vibration of the motor beneath her. They were on the move again. Turning her head, she looked out the porthole. The porthole she hadn't won but had anyway because James had given it to her without a fight.

As if she wasn't worth the fight.

But that was a problem for another day. Or, you know, never. At the moment, she needed to own her past and her mistakes—of which there were many. That's what adulting meant, right? She was going to have to face all of it. Trying to pretend to vacation while working to keep a promise to her boss. Giving her dad the divorce papers right before Christmas.

James . . .

Mad at herself, she pulled on a bathing suit and another sundress—which for someone who'd just come from the States in December felt unreal. After an extremely cold fall and early winter at home, she'd been unable to fathom ever being warm again, so she had packed heavy clothes. She added a thick cardigan sweater to her ensemble before padding upstairs.

It was a stunning Caribbean morning, already warm and glorious, which was a comfort but also made her heart hurt. Drawing a deep breath, she went directly to the closed bridge door and lifted her hand to knock.

But didn't.

Instead, she hesitated, picturing how happy her dad had been at the idea of seeing his estranged wife again.

How was she going to do this without breaking his heart? Answer: she wasn't.

Lowering her hand, she swore and turned to walk away. But . . . she couldn't. He *needed* to know. Turning back, she stared at the door again. For god's sake, make like a Nike commercial and Just Do It already. Again she tried to knock, but couldn't make her knuckles touch the wood. "Argh!" Spinning on a heel to leave, she plowed right into a brick wall.

James.

Of course. Because this wasn't hard enough.

"Whoa," he said, easily absorbing the impact without moving, wrapping his arms around her to keep her from falling.

Which was how she found herself face-first in the crook of his neck, enveloped in the only pair of arms where she'd ever felt at home. For a beat, she didn't move, didn't breathe, didn't do anything but sift her way through the memories of being right here in his arms on this boat, safe and sound and cared for.

When she didn't move, his arms tightened a bit, and he bent and put his head against hers. "You okay?"

Sure. For someone completely losing her shit.

"Hannah?"

Just the low timbre of his voice had her eyes stinging. She decided to blame this on the sun and the morning breeze, which was blowing her hair into her face.

James looked in his element in a pair of board shorts and a T-shirt advertising something in Spanish. He was warm and toasty and so familiar she burrowed in closer without thinking.

He stilled before squeezing her gently. "Hey," he said softly. "Let's go somewhere else not quite so visible."

"Why?"

"Because I know you hate it when anyone sees you cry."

She sniffed and shook her head. "I'm not crying." But she was sweating. She shucked her sweater. "It's just allergies."

"Yeah. You're allergic to confrontation," he said dryly and untangled her fingers from where, oh boy, they'd been fisted in his shirt. Taking her by the hand, he pulled her away from the bridge, portside toward the stern until they came to the aft deck. This was where guests usually hung out on the days they were moored and near land. It was half-covered, half-open to the sky, complete with a stocked bar, tables for dining, and comfortable lounge chairs, and led to the swim platform where all the toys were kept, such as snorkel gear and flotation devices—all empty now.

James gestured to the ladder that would take them up a level to the crow's nest, where they'd be two stories up in the lookout, all alone.

"I don't bite," he said. "Not unless you ask real nice."

Rolling her eyes to hide the fact that for one second she was tempted, she reached for the ladder. She started to climb, all too aware of him beneath her waiting for his turn. "Are you staring up my dress?" she asked.

"I do that only when you're *not* crying."

She snorted, then realized that somehow he'd managed to make her sadness retreat a little. At the top of the ladder, she climbed into the crow's nest, which was a round platform with a railing protecting the "nest." Someone—most likely Sally—had wrapped the mast with holly, and there was also a tiny Christmas tree that looked more like a Groot wannabe than anything else, decorated with eco-safe scrap ribbons and what looked like salt dough ornaments.

Definitely Sally's doing.

The area was small, and the farthest she could

move was maybe three feet. She was hugging herself and looking out at the stunning 360-degree view when James came up behind her.

"So . . . what's going on?"

"Nothing," she said, proud that she'd managed to collect herself.

"It's never nothing." He moved to her side and eyed the water before turning all his attention on her.

Feeling oddly vulnerable, her emotions still far too close to the surface for her comfort, she sighed. "It's complicated."

"Yes," he agreed. "Everything is."

Right. And this was James, who like it or not—and for the record, she didn't—knew her better than just about anyone else, even if they hadn't seen each other for a while. "My mom's new boyfriend proposed to her. She's got a date picked out and everything."

"Except she's already married," James pointed out.

"Right." Hannah patted the purse hanging across her body. "She's divorcing him. I've got the papers."

James let out a surprised exhale. "Jesus, Hannah, you're going to destroy the guy."

"Look, I know, okay? But she was going to have a *courier* deliver them just before he set sail yesterday, and I . . ." She shook her head. Closed her eyes. "I couldn't let him find out like that."

She heard James expel a harsh breath. "She shouldn't have let you do this for her, Hannah. She should never have put you in this position, much less this week of all weeks, over the holiday. She knew what this time means to him."

"Yeah," she murmured, eyes still closed. "I know. I also know that heartbreak wasn't on his Dear Santa list." Nope. *She'd* been the only thing there.

James lifted her chin with a finger and waited until she opened her eyes. "And I'd bet you delivering the news wasn't on yours," he said quietly.

"No. I hate knowing I'm going to hurt him."

"That's why you're here this year, so he'd at least have you when he got the news."

She looked away, not sure her being here would help at all. "Figured I was better than nothing."

"You know you are," he told her, his voice low and serious. "You're important to him."

She hoped, but wasn't all that sure sometimes.

"So she's not really joining us in Puerto Rico."

"I didn't know she was going to tell him that," she admitted. "I think he's been holding out hope for a reconciliation this whole time. Finding out that's not *ever* going to happen is going to break his heart. And not to make this about me, but I don't have any idea how to tell him."

He ran the pads of his thumbs beneath her eyes, swiping at the tears she hadn't been aware she'd let fall. "I get that. And it's not your fault, Hannah. Not the way she chose to tell him or how he chose to keep his head in the sand for so long when it comes to her. But you're here now. If I were you,

I'd do it sooner rather than later. Rip off the Band-Aid."

She met his gaze, surprised by the not-your-fault thing. Intellectually she knew that was true, but emotions were never logical, at least not for her. "I'm going to break his heart."

"Yeah, I know the feeling."

Surprised that he'd gone there, she took a deep breath. They hadn't talked about what had happened between them, indeed hadn't been sure if they ever would. But she knew she owed him an apology. "James, about—"

"What was on *your* list?" he cut her off to ask.

"What?"

"You said you doubted that divorce was on Harry's Christmas list. How about you? What's on yours?"

She paused, thrown by a question that she actually hadn't given a second's thought to. "I . . . I don't know."

"Why not?"

She shrugged. "I guess I've been so worried about this, and also underwater at work, building a case that's due to go before a judge in a few days, that I haven't even had time to think about the holidays, much less what I'd wish for."

His eyes were on hers, unreadable now, as she braced for the age-old argument between them: she worked too hard, never took the time to live her life. And while that was all true, she didn't want to fight with him. "James . . ."

He held up a finger and disappeared down the ladder.

Okay, so that'd gone pretty much as she'd expected. With a sigh, she sat on the platform, hugged her knees, and stared through the open slats of wood railing. The day was getting warmer and more humid now, each swell of the sea lit from the sun, the whitecaps sparkling like strings of twinkly infinity lights, so beautiful it took her breath away. As far as she could see there was nothing but wide-open ocean and an endless bright blue sky.

There were certainly worse places to find herself in the dead of winter. But even that didn't help all the butterflies flapping loose and fancy-free in her gut.

"Here."

James had reappeared without a sound, crouching at her side, holding something out to her in a closed fist.

She stared at his hand. "What is it?"

"A Christmas present."

"Oh." She shook her head. "But . . . I didn't—I didn't know you'd be here."

He opened his hand, palm up, revealing an exquisite anklet with dainty blue stone charms woven onto the delicate silver chain.

Recognizing it immediately, she sucked in a breath. The stone was Larimar, a rare blue variety of the mineral pectolite, unique to the region. The last time she'd been here, she'd seen it on one of the islands and it had been all she'd wanted for

Christmas that year. But neither of her parents had remembered.

Clearly James had. She stared at it, her throat thick, unsure what this meant.

"Maybe this will help get you into the holiday spirit," James said quietly.

She lifted her gaze from the anklet. "I thought you said you didn't know I was coming."

"I didn't. I saw it in a market in the Dominican Republic a few years back. I was going to give it to Harry to pass on to you." He reached over and pulled her bare foot into his lap. Then he unhooked the anklet, carefully wrapped it around her ankle, and resecured it, the feel of his warm, calloused fingers on her skin giving her a shiver.

He looked up. "Cold?"

"No," she whispered, beyond touched. "James, I didn't get you anything."

His gaze fell to her lips and he smiled. "Well, I've been mentally working up quite the list. It's pretty extensive."

She gave a shocked laugh and watched as his gaze fell to her mouth. Around them, the air was thick with regrets, longing for what had once been, and the fear of getting hurt. "James, I can't—"

"I know."

She stared down at the pretty anklet against her skin. "About that year and what happened between us . . ."

He shook his head. "Not talking about it."

"But—"

He set a gentle finger on her lips. "I'm still struggling with the fact that I'm back here on this boat without Jason." He closed his eyes for a long beat. "I'm not . . . I'm not steady enough for more today."

It felt like a knife twisted in her heart. "I'm so sorry. What can I do?"

James drew a deep breath. "You can leave the past in the past."

Just then a voice came over the loudspeaker.

"Morning, cruisers, this is your captain speaking. All guests please join me on the aft deck immediately." After a pause, the voice went on: "This means you, Smalls and WK!"

Hannah sighed and eyed James, still crouched at her side, easily balanced on the balls of his feet. "Do you think he's going to interrupt every conversation we try to have?"

"It's your dad. So yeah, probably."

Hannah found another laugh in her, and apparently James did too, and as she soaked up the sight of his quick smile, she had to remind herself not to even *think* about falling for him again. Been there, done that, and it had been more than enough heartbreak for a lifetime.

Chapter Four

JAMES HELD out a hand to Hannah and tugged her up, and okay, maybe into him just a little bit. But hell, no one had ever accused him of being smart when it came to matters of the heart. Even so, for that brief moment when she was off-balance and against him, his world stopped spinning.

And he'd like to think that little hitch in her breath meant she felt the same. Which was bad because that meant that neither of them was thinking straight, always dangerous when it came to dealing with Hannah.

She cleared her throat. "James . . ."

"Captain called," he said, and gestured for her to climb down first. Not, it should be noted, because he was a gentleman, but because if he had to watch her ass for that agonizing thirty-second climb down as he had on the way up, he wasn't sure he could keep his hands to himself.

They found Harry waiting on the aft deck, Santa hat firmly in place on top of his head, hands on hips.

"Dad?" Hannah moved to him. "What's wrong?"

"Nothing, which is a damn good thing. If it'd been a fire or some other emergency, you'd both be toast. Need to put a hitch in your giddyup, kiddos. The day's a-wasting."

Hannah blinked. "What are you talking about?"

Harry gestured dramatically behind him, where for the first time James realized they were within sight of the small private island that had been their Day Two stop on every trip he'd ever made on this ship. The island belonged to a friend of Harry's, who allowed him to use it for his guests to play on. James and his family had spent a lot of time on that tiny little oasis of sand and bluffs, his mom and dad sitting on the shoreline reading or snoozing, or just watching James and Jason and Hannah go full-out in competitive spirit at whatever they'd been up to. They'd snorkeled here, played Nerf football on the beach, climbed palm trees, and raced to the top of the bluffs to jump into the water far below . . .

So many adventures, and all of them had not only shaped James's childhood but had also fueled him to want more adventures from such an early age. It was the reason he'd finally, a year after Jason's death, started his own expedition company. He and a select group of people he'd hired worked as travel guides, taking groups out on adventures, specializing in high-end extreme vacations.

Just this year, his company had finally started to take off in a big way and he needed, *wanted*, to dedicate his time to it.

Which was why he was here. He too needed to talk to *his* dad. He'd tried a bunch of times over the past few years, but his dad, brilliant and stubborn, had managed to evade any real decision. James suspected he knew what his son wanted to talk to him about—leaving the family business for his own. So it was with no other choice that he'd come here, away from work, to get his dad's full attention. What better way than being stuck on a boat together for three to four days with no other distractions?

But he hadn't expected the biggest distraction of them all—Hannah.

"You two take the dinghy," Harry said. "Sally and I will be right behind you on the inflatable. Set up for the day while you're at it, huh? *What?*" he asked at Hannah's dry look. "Gotta earn your keep, Smalls. This is a no-dough-earned trip for me. I let Hugo and Mateo have the week off. But even with that, my baby costs big bucks to keep running. There's no such thing as a free ride. Or a free anything."

"Which is why you should've turned around when I asked," Hannah said.

"Maybe I wanted to give you a Christmas gift too."

While Hannah looked to be trying to find a comeback for that, James tugged her to the dinghy, hoping to avoid having a fight.

"Are you serious?" she asked him when they were alone.

"Would you rather stay on board all day and scrub the decks?"

He figured the point was made when she dropped into the dinghy and waited for him to jump in before untying them and starting to row.

And that was the thing about Hannah. She was no shrinking violet. She'd never been content to sit back and let someone take over for her. If there was something that had to be done, she did it. Especially if that something happened to be an adventure. He'd loved that about her. Heck, he'd loved *her*.

But in the end, he'd been alone in that.

They didn't speak. The only sounds were the sliding of the oars into the water and the slap of the swells against the hull of the dinghy.

"I'm surprised you came," she finally said.

"She speaks." And because she was sounding breathless, he reached for the oars to take over, but she shook her head and kept rowing.

"I'm surprised," she went on. "Because I imagine you're just as busy as I am, what with the two jobs."

His brows went up. "You've either been asking around about me or stalking me."

She actually blushed. It was fascinating. *She* was fascinating, damn her.

"Fine. I've kept up with you through my mom," she admitted. "She talks to your mom all the time."

He was surprised at the mixed feelings this stirred up in him. Yes, he very much enjoyed the idea of her keeping track of him. But it also pissed him off. "You could have texted, emailed, called . . . anything. I'd have told you whatever you wanted to know."

She stared at him, then looked away.

"Right." He nodded. "You didn't want to talk to me. Message received, believe me."

"That's not what the message was."

She didn't say anything else, and hell if he would ask.

Halfway to shore, she slowed, puffing for air. "I've spent . . . way too much time . . . behind a desk lately," she gasped out.

This time when he reached for the oars, she let him take them. "Do you love what you do?" he asked, genuinely curious. He wasn't sure what there could be to enjoy, being in an office all day long pushing papers.

She hesitated at the question, further piquing his interest. "I *believe* in what I do," she finally said.

He didn't want to, but he felt a pang for her regardless. For him too, and the loss of what once had been. She didn't seem . . . happy. "Hannah."

She grimaced. "Look, things change, okay? Childhood dreams change. We grow up. I grew up. Exploring the planet, chasing adventures—that was a girl's dream. What I do now works for me."

"Okay," he said.

She shook her head, stood up in the dinghy, tugged off her adorably sexy little sundress—

leaving her in a heart-stopping white bikini—and dove into the water. A perfect dive, by the way, leaving almost no splash at all.

When he pulled the dinghy up onto the sand, she was standing, hands on hips, dripping water as she stared down at a fancy spread of food and wine on a blanket in the shade between two palm trees. "Thought he told *us* to set up."

James shrugged. He'd given up trying to figure out Harry a long time ago. Most of the time he was a good guy with a short attention span when it came to anything other than the boat. But then every once in a while he did something that showed he was paying attention to the world around him beyond his own personal-space bubble.

"I think the captain fancies he's on the Love Boat," Hannah said grimly.

James opened the picnic basket, snatched an apple, and took a big bite. "At least he left us food."

She stared at him like he'd lost his mind. "Don't eat that! Don't eat anything! You'll only encourage him!" With that, she whipped around to stare at *The Therapist* and gasped.

It was moving.

Away from them.

"Be back at sunset," came Harry's voice from the loudspeaker that carried over the water.

Hannah lifted her hands in a "what the hell?" gesture at the boat.

Nothing.

She changed to a double middle finger salute.

"Saw that," Harry said from even farther away now.

James took the moment to enjoy Hannah in the bikini from the back, a sight that most likely was going to kill him. She was angry, irritated to the max, and . . . gorgeous. She bent to her sundress on the blanket, where James had set it for her, having brought it from the dinghy—nearly giving him heart failure, but it would have been a helluva way to go. Pulling her phone from the pocket, she straightened and hit a number, putting it on speaker for James to hear.

"WTF?" she said when her dad answered with a cheery "Yo!"

Harry paused. "What does WTF mean?" he asked. "No, wait, let me guess. It means . . . thank you, Father."

She glanced at him across the water. "It means *what the freak* are you up to?"

"Who, me?"

"Yeah, you, Dad. Dumping us here. This fancy spread . . . What've you been doing, taking decorating tips from *The Bachelor* marathons?"

"Hey, that was our secret," Harry said. "Look, it just seemed like you needed a little fun. Take the day, enjoy it—though that might be hard to do, since you stole your phone back—but hopefully you'll try."

"*Dad.*"

"Work can keep, Smalls. Life can't."

Hannah rubbed the crease between her eyes, looking like she was ready to blow a gasket. "You always do this to me. You put fun ahead of real life . . . Hello? *Hello?*" She looked at the screen. "Damn it. He disconnected me. Can you believe him?"

James turned and started walking along the beach.

"Where are you going?"

Instead of answering, he headed to the base of the bluffs that he knew like the back of his hand. He could hear her following him, swearing beneath her breath about the crazy people in her life and the need for a change.

James was all for change.

It took twenty minutes to get to the top, but he beat his and Jason's best time by at least five minutes. Which hurt like hell. He was standing there at the top, hand pressing against the ache in his chest, when Hannah came up beside him, breathing heavily.

He waited for a smartass comment, not entirely sure he had it in him at the moment to volley back. But she didn't say anything, wiseass or otherwise. She simply met his gaze. "You okay?" she asked softly.

"It's you who's breathing like you just ran a marathon."

"Yeah, well, desk jockey . . . You going to jump?"

He hesitated, and she turned to face him. "It's about Jason," she said softly.

"It just hit me that I've never done this without him on one side and you on the other," he admitted.

"I know." She reached for his hand. "We're missing a third of our posse." She looked into his eyes. "You're not okay."

"I'm . . ." He shook his head. "I stayed away so long . . . I think in part to avoid this. Facing it." He swallowed hard. "The truth is, I'm not quite sure how to be here without him."

"You do what needs to be done when you've got to say goodbye to someone who should still be here." Grief and sympathy in her warm eyes, still holding his hand, she stepped into him. "You live for him."

"I'm trying." He lifted his gaze to hers, not steady on his feet and extremely grateful for her presence as he realized there was no one but Hannah who could've gotten through to him in this moment. "But I feel guilty that I'm here and he isn't." He shook his head. "I've taken so many chances that I'm lucky to still be standing, and all he ever did was live his life to help my dad, and then fight like hell to stay alive for as long as it was physically possible for him to do so. It's not fair."

She tightened her grip on his hand and stared right into his eyes, her own sparkly with emotion and a few tears. "I know you miss him more than I can possibly imagine, but he wouldn't want you to feel guilty that you're still standing. He'd want you to remember the good times and think of him."

"I do," he said fiercely. He looked around. "Do

you remember that first time we stood right here? It was our third year on the boat. We were what, maybe fourteen, fifteen, and sixteen?"

She gave a small smile. "I wanted to jump, but I was scared. My dad promised he'd jump with me, but he got busy."

More like Harry had forgotten his promise to her. This happened a lot with both her parents, a fact that had always pissed him off for her. Jason and his dad had also always included her in everything they'd done. But that had been for only one week of the year. The rest of the time, she'd grown up in an unstable household that no doubt had felt unsafe, watching adults being unkind to one another and not witnessing the best of human behavior.

Which made her generosity and kindness all the more a miracle.

But on the third year of being stood up by the Cap, Jason finally sweet-talked her into joining them up the bluffs. Jason had been good at sweet talk. After promising he'd go first and be there in the water waiting for her, he jumped, and then he had indeed stayed right there in the water, waving up at her.

James had never been much of a sweet talker. When they'd been young, he and Hannah had pushed and dared and challenged each other. But now, with the dubious honor of maturity, he could care less about one-upping her, he just wanted to be with her. Terrifying in its own right.

"We going to jump?" she asked quietly.

"I am. But you don't have to."

She looked at the water, as if she wished Jason were waiting for her.

Same, babe. Same.

"You first," she finally said.

He laughed. "No can do, Hannah Banana. The second I jump, you'll walk back down."

"Yes, but that would technically still be meeting you down there," she said, biting her lower lip, staring down at the water with genuine trepidation.

Watching her, something in him softened. "If you don't want to jump," he said, "we'll both walk down."

"But you always jump. Every time. That's what we do."

"That's right. That's what *we* do."

She stared at him. "Yeah, but the adult half of this so-called *we* realizes what a stupid and idiotic tradition that is." She paused and looked down again. "I don't remember this being so scary."

"Hannah." He squeezed her hand. "We don't have to do this."

"Yes we do. Jason might be watching. Besides, I want to."

"Really? Because you look like you're going to throw up."

"I always feel this way before I jump," she said. "It's just been a long time. And . . ." She took another peek over the edge and swallowed hard. "I mean, shouldn't things look smaller when you're older? Does this cliff seem higher and bigger to you? And the waterline far lower? Global warming, right?"

He laughed and felt some of the weight lift off his chest. "It's called fear. It's okay, Hannah, seriously. We don't have to do this."

"We're doing this."

He knew that stubborn tone and that equally stubborn set of her chin. There'd be no turning back now. "Fine," he said, "then we do it together."

Staring at him, she nodded.

So they jumped.

Or more accurately, *he* jumped and she came along with him, since he was still holding her hand. And then they were flying through the air together, she screaming at the top of her lungs, the sun making her anklet glow, he feeling a ridiculous carefree grin cross his face for the first time in far too long.

Chapter Five

Hᴀɴɴᴀʜ sᴛᴏᴘᴘᴇᴅ screaming to suck in a lungful of air just before she and James hit the water. When she broke the surface, she was thrilled to find herself not dead. "Oh my god. We lived."

James, who'd surfaced at her side, laughed, looking far lighter and freer than he had at the top of the bluff.

Her heart ached for him, deeply. He and Jason had been inseparable. For her, losing Jason had felt like the hacking off of a limb, so she couldn't even fathom the pain James felt. "You didn't have to hold my hand," she said, treading water. "We're not kids anymore."

"Maybe I felt like one again."

She could tell he wasn't kidding, and that reached right into her chest and squeezed her heart. They were still treading water and staring at each other when a big swell nudged them together. His hands gripped her waist to keep her with him, their legs brushing together as he kicked to keep them afloat.

"Is this really your first time back here?" she asked.

"Yeah." He gave a small smile. "I've seen nearly every stretch of beach on the planet, but not this one, not since . . ."

"I know," she whispered, shifting closer without thought. Their thighs bumped again. Their chests too, so he tightened his grip, holding her against him.

"What made you come back this year?" she asked, her hands going to his shoulders. "Why now?"

"I told myself it was because my mom asked, and because I needed to talk to my dad, but I've gotta admit . . ." He held her gaze. "I'm glad I did."

Her heart tightened. "What about Candy?"

"She's an employee of mine," he said. "Married to one of my investment partners. They're very happy together and have an adorable little kid."

"Oh."

"Yeah. *Oh*," he said with a smile, the kind that changed the rhythm of her heart. "We were in Belize scoping out some future vacation stops, talking to some resorts willing to give us deep discounts for our clients." He lightly touched his nose to hers. "Now you."

"Now me what?"

"You still with that suit who works at a bank?"

She went brows up at him, and he smiled. "You're not the only one who gets gossip from a parent. Our moms are still like two middle school girls."

She laughed. "Yeah. They are."

"So. The suit?"

She met his warm but curious gaze. "He was too . . . suity."

He laughed, and the sound woke up all her good parts. Looking at him, she could almost feel the forces of gravity shift from pulling her under the water to pushing her even closer to James in the hope that he might kiss her. Just thinking about it had her gaze dropping to his mouth.

Maybe he felt the same pull because he said her name in a low sexy timbre that wasn't technically a question but sure felt like one.

She answered with a nod and a "yes, please," and then his mouth was on hers. Not forcefully, but with enough intensity that she could feel the promise behind the kiss, along with the promise of much more if she wanted it.

And in that moment, there wasn't *anything* she wanted other than more—more of this, more of him, more of *them* . . . All of which she tried to convey with her kiss, something he returned with a heat and hunger that stole her breath. He had one hand fisted in her hair, the other low on her back pressing her against him as his legs continued to work at keeping them afloat. He pulled back, studied her face, and then smiled.

And then she kissed that smile off his face.

When they started to slide underwater, he kicked them back to the surface, both of them coughing and laughing.

By mutual silent agreement, they began to swim to shore. Which of course turned into a race and then a dunking contest. When they stepped out of the water, still cracking up, they made their way through the stuff Harry had left for them, which included a Nerf football. While they tossed it back and forth, Hannah worked on doing something she rarely accomplished anymore—staying in the moment *and* enjoying it.

Although she thought of herself as a natural athlete, she hadn't flexed those muscles in a while. It'd been a long time since she'd thrown a ball, yet she could still get it to James—well, in his vicinity at least. He was a good sport, running and diving for her errant tosses in nothing but board shorts hanging dangerously low on his sexy hips. Of course he was able to get the ball right into her hands. Tired now, but also determined, she gave the ball one last toss just to see him run. He hurled himself into the air to make the catch, then hit the sand hard and stayed down. And still—way too still.

"Oh my god," she whispered and ran over to him. "James?"

Nothing.

She dropped to her knees and put her hand on his bare back. His skin was smooth and warm. *"James!"*

He moved so fast she never saw him coming. In the next breath, she was flat on her back and he was braced above her, mischief in his gaze.

"I take it you're done playing football," she managed, her pulse kicking into gear. He was big and warm and hard. *Everywhere.*

"Babe, that wasn't football. You were too busy ogling me to even try and throw it the way I taught you."

She bit her lower lip and stared at his mouth. "You're too . . . tempting."

"Is that a problem?"

"I don't know yet."

He smiled, lowered his head until his lips touched hers, and then finally kissed her until her toes started to curl and she was panting and trying to get inside his bathing suit.

Which was when he rose to his feet and headed back to their picnic area.

"Are you serious?" she asked his back.

"Thought I'd wait until you were sure you wanted to be tempted."

"That wasn't tempting me," she called after him. "That was provoking me into a huge . . . state."

He sat and began to eat a sandwich as he looked at her curiously. "What kind of state is this, exactly?"

Blowing her hair out of her face, she waited for her heart rate to slow down from stroke level. "Never you mind."

He grinned. "You can take it back, you know, and just admit you want me."

Over her dead body. She plopped down in front of the basket and accepted the sandwich he handed her. She was all too aware of her phone vibrating on the blanket. It'd been vibrating on and off since they'd gotten here. After an internal debate, she gave an apologetic smile and answered. Work, of course, and it took a bit to get everything handled, but finally she disconnected. "Sorry."

"That thing's been going off since you stepped onto *The Therapist*. Is work always this intense?"

"Usually it's worse. This is my boss showing restraint."

They had wine chilling in a cooler, and when she pulled out ridiculously fancy glasses, a few rose petals fell out as well.

James laughed. She did not. "*Nothing* about this is anything like the hot dogs and s'mores that we used to get." She shook her head. "He's upped his game."

James touched his glass to hers. "That he has."

"I'm sorry your parents aren't here for this."

He shrugged, and she set her glass down, alerted by something in his carefully blank face. "So . . . what made you come this year?"

"Maybe it was for this," he said, gesturing between them with his wineglass. "After all, Christmas wouldn't be Christmas without someone calling me on my shit every five seconds."

"Aw," she said with a laugh, "you missed this."

"Yeah, I missed this." He set his glass down. "And you," he added, surprising her. "I missed you."

Her heart fluttered, but her brain was afraid to believe. "Right. That's why when you first arrived, you looked like you were dreading this trip."

His smile faded. "That wasn't about you."

"What was it about?"

"Long story."

She lifted her hands and gestured around them. "Literally, nowhere else to go or to be."

James looked at her for a long beat. "My dad had always groomed Jason to take over the lumber business. Growing up, I was the . . . spare."

She made a sound of regret for him, but he shook his head. "I was okay with that, believe me. I never wanted to stay in New York and run the company. I always wanted to leave and explore, to find my own thing that suited *me*. But then Jason died and the spare was pulled into play. You know I took off first, needing some time. I told myself it was my nature, but the truth was, I knew if I stayed in one place too long, I'd have to face the fact that Jason was really gone."

"James," she said softly, pained.

"I came back, and ever since then I've tried to run both sides of my life at the same time, helping Dad while keeping my own business afloat too. I gave it everything I had, but I've known the truth for a long time. I'm never going to be happy fulfilling my dad's dream. I've tried to break it to him gently, but he's not hearing me. That's what this trip was for. So you're not the only one here with a mission. I've got a clock running, counting down the time until my dad catches up to us so I can tell him I want out. That the many years of grooming his sons to take over the family business were all for nothing."

"Maybe he'll understand. He's a good man. I bet what he wants more than anything is for you to be happy."

"Actually, what he wants is for me to be Jason," James said. "But I'm not him. I can't be. Not that it matters, because if my dad *really* needed me, I'd put my all into it in a heartbeat. But the thing is, he's got a great team. He doesn't actually *need* me there."

"What about you?" she asked, feeling for him in a big way. The desire not to disappoint one's parents is intense, even greater for James because of the loss of Jason. "What do *you* need?"

He looked surprised at the question, like maybe no one had ever asked him what he needed, which had her heart swelling until it felt too big for her rib cage.

"I need to be doing *my* thing," he said quietly. "Running the expedition company has never felt like work to me. I can't imagine not doing it. But splitting my focus is starting to affect both businesses."

"How in the world have you been managing to do both? It must be killing you."

"It's taken a lot of juggling. And now my company's growing faster than I can keep up with for the hours I can put into it. I just signed a huge corporate account that'll keep me busy for the immediate future, and Google's looking at me to be in charge of their team-building adventures. They want me to take their executive team to Madagascar as a test."

She smiled, unbelievably proud of him. "Congrats, that's huge. How much of this does your dad know?"

"None of it."

She blinked. "Wait, so you've known how you felt for . . . five years, and you haven't said a word?"

"I've tried to say many words."

"Okay, but now you're just going to drop the bomb on him here that the status quo no longer makes you happy and that's it, you're out? You walk away without looking back?"

He let a stunned beat of silence go by before asking quietly, "Why do I have the feeling we're no longer talking about me and my dad, but about your mom?"

She covered her face. "I'm sorry. I'm not judging you. I'm . . . confused."

He pulled her hands down, forcing her to look at him. "By this?"

"Yes." She searched for the right words. "For me, happiness isn't jumping off a cliff. For me, Vacation Happiness isn't real."

"*Everything* we do is real, Hannah. It's all a part of life."

"My life isn't like yours."

"I know."

She looked at him, chest aching. "At the end of

the day, we're two very different people who want very different things out of life. Which is why I left six years ago."

"And here I thought you ran because you were scared."

This had her sucking in a breath because . . . well, because it was actually accurate. She could still remember making love with him for the first time that Christmas. The next morning he'd sat up, said he was going to go explore the world and wanted her to go with him. Essentially, he'd wanted her to give up her scholarship, her internship . . . everything. On a whim.

But she'd known she couldn't maintain a relationship and get where she wanted to professionally, where she *needed* to go. She wanted stability and a steady future, unlike the one she'd had growing up with parents who'd each had their own agenda. "Not all of us have the luxury of doing whatever we want."

"It's a choice, Hannah. I work hard, but I also want to live hard, and I don't see why I can't do both."

"You make it sound so simple."

"Because it is," he said.

"It's not like I don't *choose* to be happy," she said. "But it's not what drives me. My work drives me."

He looked at her for a long moment. "Maybe you should tell me what's going on at work. What is it about this case that has you and your boss working around the clock?"

Once upon a time they'd told each other everything. Just as once upon a time, they'd been magic together. If that hadn't changed—and given the sheer magnitude of their chemistry, it hadn't—then she could tell him anything. She knew that. But this . . . this was going to hit him hard. "Are you sure?" she asked. "It might be difficult to hear."

His eyes held her, serious, solemn. "Lay it on me."

"I'm advocating for a patient who needs her fifteenth surgery on her heart. She's four. Her insurance company refused to approve the surgery because there's only a forty percent chance of her survival. But to her parents, forty percent is everything." She met his gaze, knowing she was telling him a story his family had also been through. "She needs the surgery to live, James."

He got to his feet and walked to the water.

Her gut sank as she took in the breadth of his shoulders and the weight on them. Because Jason had died according to this *exact* scenario—waiting on insurance approval.

Chapter Six

JAMES STOOD at the water's edge looking out at . . . nothing. Normally just the soothing sound of the waves lapping at the shore would lower his heart rate and blood pressure, but not this time. His heart was pounding in his ears, the blood rushing through his veins. Because of Jason, yes. But also for Hannah. Here he'd always believed she'd misunderstood him, but he'd been the one to misunderstand *her*.

She came up at his side, her bare feet sinking into the wet sand, her loose brunette waves blowing around her face.

"I had no idea," he said quietly. "No idea what you actually did, what your job entailed. It's . . . incredible." He reached for her hand, turning her to face him. "You're incredible." When her eyes went shiny, he pulled her closer. "I've always thought that, Hannah, with or without your job, but even more so now. You're changing lives, making sure that some people get to live a healthier, longer life than they would've otherwise."

She nodded and gave him a small smile, which

he helplessly returned. "So I guess you were hoping to hand deliver a pretty big Christmas present to the girl's family this week," he said. "Instead your boss gets to."

"Assuming we win. Only, as you know, that's never a given." She paused, as if searching for the right words. "It's always great when I get to see the looks on their faces, but in the end, it doesn't matter who delivers the news. All that matters is that the patient gets what they need."

He shook his head, still marveling at her. "How did you end up with a job like that? Your degree was in business. You started out at a bank, right?"

"I did." She met his gaze. "But after watching what your family suffered and struggled through with Jason's health, I knew I wanted to do something else. I kept the bank job while I looked around. It took me a couple of years, but when the position for health care advocate at my local hospital opened up, I applied."

He felt overwhelmed by her revelation. That last Christmas they'd spent together had been only a few months after Jason had died. He'd been messed up and hard on everyone, especially Hannah. He didn't like to look back on that time because it made him feel like there was an elephant sitting on his chest, but memories were coming in fast and hot now.

He'd been so caught up in his own grief and issues that he'd overlooked that she too had loved and lost Jason. Her parents were split up by then, and all of this had hit her hard as well, but none of it had stopped her. While he'd been running from continent to continent and then building his business, not dealing with his grief, Hannah had chosen to make a difference by working with families just like his every day.

So really, who had let whom down? "Hannah—"

"Look." She pointed out at the water, where they could see *The Therapist* setting anchor.

"Ahoy!" rang out across the water.

Captain Harry, with his impeccable timing.

Chapter Seven

Much later that night back on the ship, Hannah was helping her dad hang some new sparkling holiday lights that he'd not yet gotten up. Her mind kept drifting, playing the day on repeat—jumping off the bluffs, kissing James . . .

I thought you ran because you were scared . . .

"Well, if that's not a crock of french fried baloney," she muttered to herself, even *knowing* there'd actually been a lot of truth to his statement. She *had* hidden behind her scholarship and internship, when the truth was, what she'd had with James had been more real than anything else in her life, and well worth fighting for.

Something she'd never told him.

Harry stopped trying to untangle a ball of electrical cord and looked at her. "What are you muttering about?"

"Nothing." She paused. "Love is dumb."

He laughed and wobbled as he climbed a ladder, making her gasp and wrap her arms around the ladder and the bottoms of his legs. "Dad!"

"I'm fine."

Sure. He was fine. And three sheets to the wind as well. "Seriously, please let one of us do this for you."

"Are you kidding me? Trust my baby to a youngster?"

Of course the boat was his baby. It certainly wasn't her—she wasn't even his real daughter. Even though he'd raised her since she was a toddler, she always knew where she stood in the lineup. When it came to Harry, his priorities went: boat, fun, family—meaning her mom—and then finally Hannah.

She'd always understood that, accepted that, and even understood that was why James and Jason and their parents had been so important to her.

But sometimes deep down, when she let herself think about it too long, it stirred up feelings inside her she didn't like. She was jealous of a damn boat. "Dad, you always trusted one of your 'youngster' crew to watch me when I was little."

"Well, that's different, kiddo. The boat needed my attention more than you did."

Hannah sucked in a breath just as someone came up behind her. Turning, she met James's gaze, warm with concern.

"You okay?" he asked quietly.

Embarrassed without really understanding why, she nodded.

James looked up at her dad. "How about you come down before you hurt anyone else?"

"What are you talking about? I'd never hurt my boat."

"Yeah, I was talking about your daughter. Come

on." And then, without waiting for Harry to agree, James moved close enough to reach up and take ahold of the back of Harry's shirt. "Slowly."

Harry sighed. "I'm not an invalid." But as he backed down the ladder, he missed the second-to-last rung and would've fallen if James hadn't been standing there to steady him.

On the deck, Harry scrubbed a hand over his face. "I've made a mess of this."

James set a hand on her dad's shoulder. "Go sleep it off."

Harry nodded, then paused. "Thanks, James."

James looked surprised as he met Harry's gaze, probably because in all these years, she didn't think her dad had ever called James by his given name. He had always referred to him as WK. She'd always figured that was her dad's way of reminding James that he still thought of him as a kid.

Harry nodded at them both and walked off.

James stepped closer and tilted her face up to his. "I'm going to ask you again. You okay?"

"Yeah. That was just Harry being Harry."

"He'd been drinking."

"Yes, which makes him even more stubborn than usual," she said. "Don't worry, Vacation Harry is much nicer and easier to deal with. He'll show up when your parents do."

"Hannah . . . you deserve Vacation Harry as Everyday Harry."

She shrugged and moved to walk off, but he caught her hand and slowly, almost gently, reeled her in, entangling their fingers together. "About today . . ."

"What about it?"

"I know we're two very different people," he said, carrying on their earlier conversation like no time had gone by. "But we've got the important stuff in common."

She stared into his Caribbean eyes and saw the depth of his emotions there. He was letting her in, letting her see everything: his hopes, his dreams, his pain, even the truth about how he felt for her. It all made her heart squeeze hard. "James, how we feel about each other has never been the problem."

He gave a small smile and brought her hand up to his mouth, brushing a kiss across her palm. "No, it hasn't."

Slowly, regretfully, she pulled free. "I guess I'll see you tomorrow."

"When are you going to tell your dad about the divorce?"

The nerves in her belly took flight again. "I was going to do it tonight, but obviously that didn't work out. I need to do it before the day we dock in Puerto Rico and meet up with your parents."

He nodded slowly. "Do you want company when you tell him?"

"You'd be with me?"

"Always."

It wasn't just the word, but the way he said it, voice low and serious. He had her back in a way no one else ever had.

"Let's have breakfast in the morning," he said. "We'll figure out the best way to tell him."

She nodded, and he climbed the ladder, hanging the lights with no problem, his T-shirt stretched tight over his shoulders and biceps as he moved, his long legs affording him an easy reach. His body was a finely honed machine that spoke of long days of rowing, climbing, or pursuing his latest adventure, those board shorts of his lovingly cupping a world-class—

"You're staring at my ass," he said, voice laced with amusement.

"Figured it was only fair."

He laughed softly as he climbed back down the ladder. And then he suddenly turned, putting them toe to toe, thigh to thigh. Chest to chest . . .

His hands came up and cupped her face as he slowly drew her mouth to his, giving her plenty of time to back away if she wanted.

She didn't. In fact she leaned in breathlessly as he kissed her, softly at first, teasing her a little before gently taking her bottom lip between his teeth. She moaned and clutched for purchase in a spinning world, twining her arms around his neck as he fisted his hands in her hair, kissing her hungrily now. When they finally broke apart for air, she stared at him. "Why does that just get better and better?"

He gave her a crooked smile. "One of life's little mysteries, I guess."

She stared at him, knowing she needed to walk

away now or she wasn't going to walk away at all. "I should probably go get some work done."

Nodding, he took her hand and walked with her.

"What are you doing?" she asked.

"Walking you to your room."

"This isn't a date."

He smiled again. "Feels like one whenever I'm with you."

She stared into his eyes and then lowered her gaze to his mouth.

He groaned softly. "Hannah. I want to kiss you when you look at me like that."

"Good, because I *want* you to kiss me."

With a rough laugh, he pulled her to him and did just that until they'd both lost themselves. "Tell me this doesn't feel like a date to you too," he murmured.

They didn't see eye to eye on . . . well, almost anything, but there was an undeniable heart and soul connection with him unlike anything else she'd ever experienced. "Maybe," she admitted. "But I'm out of dating practice, so . . ."

"Don't overthink it."

"Hi, have you met me?"

He smiled, then leaned in and kissed her on the cheek, making her realize they were in front of their rooms. "Good night," he murmured.

She absolutely wanted one. A *good night*, that was. His door was closest, so she caught his hand and tugged him inside to ensure one.

Chapter Eight

JAMES FOUND himself up against his bedroom door, an incredibly sexy and determined woman holding him there, her lips making their way down his jaw toward his mouth. The rest of his body went on high, hopeful alert. "Hannah."

"Hmm?" she murmured, mouth busy.

"I don't usually put out on the first date."

She gave a throaty laugh, as if amused by his thick voice and the way he could barely speak with her mouth on him. "Feels like we've been dating forever."

"It started in the seventh grade," he said. "You showed up with that new cute haircut."

"I thought maybe it was eighth grade, when I showed up with boobs."

He smiled, holding her tight against him. "Yeah. Maybe. Eighth-grade boys are assholes."

She took her mouth off him and met his gaze. "Why did we never admit we crushed on each other?"

He stared at her. "Wait, you're serious? You crushed on me?"

"Hard," she admitted. "Come on. I followed you around and pretended to want to do stupid boy stuff just to get your attention."

He shook his head, his brain not in gear. "Stupid boy stuff?"

"Yeah, like when you all caught fish and you were gutting them to cook for dinner, remember that?"

"Of course. You were great at it."

She shook her head. "When we were done, I staggered to the back of the boat where no one could see me and threw up."

"Hannah . . ." He laughed softly, full of sympathy. "How long until you got used to prepping the fish?"

"How many times did we have to gut them?" she asked.

"We must have done that, like, what? Ten years in a row."

"Then ten." She looked at him. "You really didn't know how I felt about you?"

He gave a small, disgusted-with-himself shake of his head. All of this was news to him. What an idiot he'd been. "Never. I always thought it was about Jason for you."

"No," she whispered, giving him a delicious shiver. Or maybe that was her mouth, making its wicked way up to his ear now, which she nipped, pulling a rough groan from him. "It was always you, James. Always." She pulled back and looked into his eyes. "I've had a crush on you since that first Christmas, but it didn't really take hold until I was fourteen and my dad taught us to drive the boat, wanting us to know how to handle ourselves in an emergency. I was terrified I'd kill us all, but he just kept saying that there was no crying on the boat. You came over and held my hand."

He remembered. She'd been so frightened, and he'd been pissed at Harry, who'd been clueless, treating her like any other crew member. Hannah had been shaking too hard to get a good grip on the helm, so he'd helped her.

"You made me feel . . . protected," she said. "Safe. Like you wouldn't let anything happen to me. Like you thought I was special."

"You are," he said, intensely enough to have her looking surprised. He was starting to realize just how scarred she'd been by two well-meaning but clueless parents, people who were supposed to love her and put her first, but who instead somehow always made her feel like an afterthought.

He'd been no better, expecting her to dump everything she knew and loved to travel the world with him—no plan, no safety net.

He'd been a selfish asshole.

"You actually fell into the water that day on purpose," Hannah said. "To show me it wasn't scary. Then you climbed back on board and held my hand."

He nodded and slid his hand into her hair to tip her face up to his. "Yeah, but that's not all I was thinking about back then."

"No? What else were you thinking about?"

He smiled and lifted her up against him, groaning when she climbed him like a tree. "The same thing I'm thinking about now."

"Which is?" she asked breathlessly.

"Some things are better suited for show, not tell."

When she smiled at him, he felt like he'd just won a pot of gold.

HANNAH was feeling a little bit like how she'd felt earlier when jumping off the bluffs with James. Adventurous. Exhilarated. But there was more too. A lot more.

James let her body slide down his with a delicious, electric friction before pinning her to the door in much the same way she'd done to him only moments ago.

"Showing is good," she whispered.

Their gazes met and held until James lowered his head and kissed her with a hunger that matched her own, until they were practically having sex while still fully dressed, up against the wall.

"James," she finally gasped, "I can't stand up anymore."

He lifted her off her feet and she wrapped her legs around him as he headed toward the bed.

"I've missed this with you," she confessed, mouth on his sexy throat.

"Yeah?"

"When you boarded the other day and looked at me, my heart stopped. I couldn't imagine you ever wanting me again."

"I never stopped, Hannah. Can't you feel it?"

She rocked against an impressive erection, and he let out a sexy laugh. "Not just with your body, babe. Inside, in your heart. Feel how much I want you, *all* of you."

She stared at him, seeing the truth in his eyes, and it freed her somehow. Wriggling free, she beamed at him. He smiled back, letting out a surprised laugh when she gave him a shove to the bed. He lay back on his elbows, eyes hot as he watched her crawl up his body. "Feeling aggressive?" he asked mildly.

"I'm feeling something." She tugged his shirt up, and when he took his hands from her to help pull the shirt over his head, she took advantage, leaning in to kiss her way across his yummy chest. As she headed south, he made a rough male noise and stopped her.

"Be sure, Hannah."

He was looking at her as if she was the most important thing in his entire world. "I am," she said. "I've never been more sure."

As if that had been what he'd been waiting for, he rolled them, tucking her beneath him, pinning her to the bed.

"Your turn?" she asked breathlessly.

"Yeah. My turn." His body was hard and muscular and felt so good against hers. "Pretty," he said of her sundress, and nudged the spaghetti straps down her elbows, baring her to the waist. He smiled at her breasts. "Even prettier."

She was busy trying to get his shorts off, but his clever hands were working on driving her crazy, and it was a short drive. Then he completely derailed her when he went on a southbound tour of her body. With his mouth.

"*Mmm*," he murmured, pushing the skirt of her dress up. "Hold that for me."

She mindlessly grabbed the material, and then in the next breath gasped, her head thrown back on his pillow as he slid off her panties, kissed her ankle just above the anklet he'd put on her, and then proceeded north to have his merry way with her.

She was still trying to find her way back to her own body when he lifted his head, bracing himself on his forearms above her. Reaching up, she entangled her hands in his hair and tugged him to her.

With a rough groan, he kissed her wildly until she was once again on the very edge, and then he produced a condom—thank god one of them was thinking—and finally slid home.

Breathless, heart pounding, she gazed up at him to find him staring right back at her, clearly just as moved. She drew a shaky breath. "I don't get how you do this to me."

"It's you, Hannah." His voice was husky. "It's all you. You're amazing. And you make me feel . . ."

"What?" She was struggling now for words, but

she wanted to know. *Needed* to know. "I make you feel . . . what?"

"*Everything,*" he said roughly, a warm hand caressing one side of her neck and throat while his lips nuzzled the other side. Then he began to move, a slow, torturous grind, head back, eyes closed, sheer undiluted pleasure in every line of his face. When he opened his eyes and whispered her name, she lost herself in him, completely.

Just as when she was with him like this, she also felt . . . found.

Chapter Nine

JAMES OPENED his eyes, and in spite of the fact that Hannah had just blown his mind and melted all his bones, he managed to lift his head and run a finger along her temple, tucking a stray strand of hair from her eyes so he could see into them. "Hey," he murmured.

She smiled lazily, looking so sated it boosted his ego. "Hey," she murmured back.

He smiled. "Wish I could go back and tell teenage James that being with you is even better than I imagined. And trust me, I imagined a lot."

That won him a laugh, which with Hannah felt like a huge victory. He knew there wasn't much light in her world, and if he couldn't change that, he could at least make her feel as good as he possibly could. To that goal, he nibbled his way to her mouth, and was kissing her and loving the little breathy whimpers for more when a sudden knock had her nearly leaping right out of his arms. "Shh," he murmured, running his hands up and down her back. "It's okay."

"It's not okay!" she whispered back, eyes wide. "You know who that probably is!"

And indeed, Harry's voice came through the door. "See you at dawn for fishing, yeah?"

"Yep," James called out, trying not to laugh because Hannah had dived beneath the covers. "First thing."

"Okay then. Night, James." He paused. "Night, Smalls."

Hannah tugged the blanket off her face, grimaced, then called out, "Night, Dad."

After her dad's footsteps had faded away, she sat up. "Oh my god. If our moms were here, they'd already be planning our wedding."

James snorted because that was true.

"This isn't funny. He's going to think we're a *we* now."

"Probably." James kissed his way down her throat. "What's wrong with that?"

"Right this moment?" she asked breathlessly, moaning when he added his hands to the fray. "Absolutely nothing."

LATER, they dozed, wrapped up in each other. At some point, James awoke with a smile on his face and couldn't remember ever feeling so relaxed and happy. At the odd movement next to him, he cracked open an eye and found Hannah sitting up beside him, working on her phone. Stretching, he slid an arm across her and tucked her into him.

She didn't even look over, just kept typing while also giving a huge, jaw-cracking yawn.

Huh. Guess he was alone in that relaxed and happy state. "How long have you been up?"

"Oh, I haven't gone to sleep yet." She yawned again, looking completely done in.

"I could've sworn you fell asleep after that last orgasm."

She smiled. "Yeah, and thanks for those, by the way. It's been a while. Sorry if I was rusty."

"You were perfect." He kissed her shoulder. "You really haven't slept?"

"No, I waited for you to fall asleep so I wouldn't bug you."

He lifted his head and met her gaze. "That wouldn't bug me. What does is your working in the middle of the night when you're exhausted and could use some rest."

"I'm not exhausted—" She broke off for yet another yawn and then flushed. "Okay, so I'm a little tired."

"You mean dead on your feet."

She smiled ruefully. "I've got to do this. These are a few new cases I'm getting preliminary info together for that I'll need right after the New Year."

He nodded, starting to catch on. It'd taken him long enough. "There's always going to be another patient, isn't there?"

"Well, yeah," she said, sparing him a quick glance. "It's the nature of the job, which is what I love about it."

"Because it allows you to bury yourself in work and never really live for yourself?"

Again she looked up, this time with a small frown. "I thought you understood."

"Because of what happened to Jason?"

"Yes."

He nodded, but then slowly shook his head. "No. Jason had regrets, Hannah—so many regrets. In the end, he was angry at himself for not living his life for anything beyond the job. I'd hate that for you."

"I don't have regrets." She paused and let her phone fall into her lap. "Look, I know it's a holiday week and most people are off from work, but today's going to be busy and my boss will probably need my help. But believe me, I get your frustration. It's an impossible situation, and why I don't really date. It's too hard to juggle it all, and in the end I always feel forced to choose between my job and a guy."

"So you chose the job?"

"Well, yeah," she said. "Because it's easier than facing the fact that I'm never quite . . . enough for someone."

Damn. She always got him right in the gut. "Hannah, you're more than enough."

"Am I, though? Because you'd like me to change. You'd like me to set down this phone and maybe have a repeat of what we did earlier."

That brought a brief smile to his lips. "Never doubt that. But that's not what this is about."

"Working hard is a source of pride for me, James. It's all I know."

He knew this was true. She'd basically raised her mom and stepdad, both of whom were decent people, but also selfish and at times incredibly immature. He had no idea how to make that any different for her. He couldn't change the past, but maybe he could help Future Hannah, even if just a little. "You're tired," he said quietly. "Why don't you get a couple of hours' sleep?"

She nodded agreeably but picked her phone back up. "In a few minutes, I promise."

He lay back and waited. Ten minutes went by. Then another ten. After thirty more, he slipped out of bed, pulled on his clothes, and left.

All without her so much as looking up.

Chapter Ten

HANNAH WAS so good at hyperfocusing that she could completely tune out her surroundings, and she did so—until she heard the door close. Blinking, she looked around.

The bed had been decimated.

And James had left.

The thought gave her a pang. As usual, she'd lost track of time. She needed to go after him, and would. Soon as she finished up this one last work email.

Only that didn't happen.

What did happen was that she came awake a few hours later with a gasp. She'd fallen asleep. It was now eight in the morning and she had a crick in her neck from sleeping half sitting up, nose in her phone. But as for the rest of her body, she had no complaints there, because she was deliciously boneless, thanks to James's careful attentiveness. Just thinking about it kicked her pulse back into gear.

Knowing they'd agreed to have breakfast on the deck, she jumped out of bed, took a quick shower, and dressed, then hurried up the stairs.

The day was stunning. Turquoise waters stretched as far as the eye could see, still and crystal clear. The air was thick and warm. The only sounds were the occasional squawks of seabirds and the gentle lap of water against the hull. As she took it all in, her heart rate slowed and she took a deep, relaxed breath. How she'd ever forgotten how beautiful it was out here, she had no idea.

Making her way to the galley, she smiled in surprise at Sally, who was at the sink.

"Hey," Hannah said, "it's my turn to make breakfast. What would you like?"

"Too late," Sally said with a wink and a smile. "I've got everything almost ready. Food's plated and covered and on a table on the aft deck."

Hannah kissed Sally on the cheek and made her way to the aft deck, stopping short at the table set romantically for two. With a sigh, she slid a look to Sally, who'd followed her out with a pitcher of orange juice. "There are no secrets on this ship."

"None," the woman said with a laugh as she walked off.

Hannah sat and waited for James, surprised that he hadn't beaten her here. He loved breakfast. Actually, he loved all food, and he was a definite morning person.

But he didn't show. She knew he wasn't in bed, since *she'd* been in it until twenty minutes ago. She started to go look for him, but her phone rang. Work. After a ten-minute call, she texted James: *you okay?*

Her dad came out from the bridge and sat down. "Hey there." He lifted the lid on her still-untouched breakfast and stole her sourdough toast.

"Hey," she said.

"You know there are only two kinds of people on this boat. The quick . . . and the hungry."

"Uh-huh," she said dryly. Her phone was buzzing, so she stole a quick look at it, hoping it was James.

It wasn't.

"So . . . " Her dad looked oddly uncomfortable. "Uh . . . nice weather, right?"

"Yes." It took her a moment to realize his dilemma. He wanted to ask how she was, but didn't want to hear about last night with James.

Since she didn't want to tell him any more than he wanted to hear about it, she decided to take the lead. "How are you?"

"Great," he said.

Great. He felt good and she felt weighed down by the divorce papers still in her cabin. "So."

"So," he said with a nod.

She sighed. "Look, this is dumb. Let's just get this over with. You were drinking pretty heavily last night."

"We were anchored. I needed to blow off some steam."

"Okay . . ." So there wasn't going to be an apology. "How was fishing? Have you seen James?"

"Yeah, and the fishing was great. We caught dinner. Oh, and he told me about his plans to expand. He said I could be one of his subcontractors. He'd book boating adventures using *The Therapist* when he could. He's dealing with high rollers, so the profit margin would be amazing."

"Dad, Mom told me recently that your doctor had asked you to think about slowing down, maybe even selling and retiring. High blood pressure, remember? And clearly the responsibility gets to you, at least sometimes." Like last night . . .

He waved this off just as her phone buzzed again.

"Should have left that thing in my hat," Harry said.

She blew out a breath. "It's my boss, Cynthia. Should only take a sec."

Harry was sipping his coffee when she finished the call. "Sorry," she said to Harry. "There might be some more of that today. The case I've been working on is going before a judge later. Everything's ready, but I'll want to find out how it went."

He nodded. "I like listening to you. You're smart, capable. Your work is important to you."

"Yes."

He nodded again. "This boat and the ocean are important to me in the same way. I'm not going to stop any more than you're going to stop trying to save the world."

She sighed. "I get it."

James appeared, wearing another pair of board shorts, these a dark navy blue paired with a white T-shirt that read *May the Fish Be with You!*

Harry pulled a ten from his pocket and waved it at him. "You were right. Your black grouper was bigger by half a pound. Bragging rights are all yours."

James grinned. "Good to know."

"Where were you?" Hannah asked him.

He turned to look at her, his eyes behind dark sunglasses, his thoughts hidden. "Figured you were working."

"Oh, she was," Harry said ever so helpfully.

"We were going to meet for breakfast," Hannah said. "I took a quick call while I was waiting, that's all."

Which was, of course, when her damn phone began to vibrate again, having a seizure on the table.

James raised a brow.

Harry gave a cough and laughed into his hand.

Hannah stared at the two men in her life as the epiphany hit her in the face. She'd been on both of them about *their* lifestyle choices, and yet here she was right before Christmas, living at the whim of her phone. "Pot, meet kettle," she muttered beneath her breath.

"What was that, Smalls?"

Before she could answer, Sally called out from the bridge with a question. Her dad got up to have that conversation, and Hannah tucked her phone away.

"What if you miss something?" James said.

That was the crux of it. She *was* missing

something—life. And it wasn't like she could do anything more for today's hearing. "Work can wait a bit," she said.

For the first time since she'd been in James's arms the night before, he met her gaze, pushing his sunglasses to the top of his head to give her a small but utterly genuine smile that warmed her from toes to roots. He leaned in and put his mouth to her ear. "That's the sexiest thing you've ever said to me."

"I thought telling you about my crush on you was pretty sexy."

"You're right. Scratch that. *Everything* you say is sexy."

"Welp." Harry came back to the table but didn't sit. "I'm off. I got stuff to do."

"Wait," Hannah said. "Can we talk later?"

"What were we just doing?"

Hannah grimaced. "I've got more to talk about."

Harry sighed. "I'm not retiring, Smalls. Period. Now, it's almost Christmas. We pick up our families in San Juan tomorrow. Fun only for the rest of the trip, you hear me?"

"Come on," she said slowly. "How realistic is that?"

"I suppose about as realistic as your being here as my gift," he said. "See you two later. Enjoy your breakfast." He looked at Hannah. "Or at least try." And with that, he headed off to the galley.

Hannah looked at James.

He shrugged. "Maybe he suspects the truth, in

which case another few hours in denial before you crush him won't hurt. Besides, have you not seen the way Sally looks at him?"

"Yeah, but he doesn't look at her that way."

James nudged a chair back from the table with a foot and sat. "Given the news you're here to deliver, maybe you can help him start to look at her that way."

"He needs to sell the boat."

He gave her a get-real look. "This boat is his life. What would he do without it?"

Hannah leaned forward. "Listen, you might not have heard, but he's had a couple of health scares. Him being out here, far from medical care, drinking at night like he is . . . My biggest fear is that something will happen when he's out here alone."

"Have you asked him what *his* biggest fear is? Because I'd bet it's being landlocked with nothing to do. He loves the water, Hannah. Lives for it."

She sagged back and sighed. "I know. He loves it above all else." *Including me . . .* "I just don't want to lose him."

"I understand that," he said. "Maybe more than anyone, but living for the sake of living isn't going to cut it, not for a guy like him."

Their gazes met, his hooded from her now. "James, what's going on?"

"What do you mean?"

"You blew me off this morning."

"To be honest, I wasn't sure if you'd notice whether I was here or not."

She was dumbstruck. "What are you talking about?"

"Last night I barely had the condom off before you had your phone in hand. Let's just say I got the message."

"I just needed to get something done before I could go to sleep, is all."

He shook his head. "I waited at least thirty minutes before I headed out. You didn't even notice I was gone."

"I'm so sorry." She drew in a breath, embarrassed. "I did hear you go. I promised myself I'd go after you the minute I finished an email, but I fell asleep. You could've said something when you left."

"Let's just say you were focused, and not on me."

"Okay," she said, nodding, because if she was being honest, she'd heard this sort of thing before from . . . well, just about every guy she'd ever dated. "I'm single-minded. I can work on that."

He gave her an unreadable look. "Your job's important to you, Hannah, and it should be. I love how passionate you are. But last night . . . it felt special to me." He paused and made sure he had her attention. "*Really* special. Then I realized I was in it alone."

She felt the air leave her lungs in a whoosh, and she stood, moving around the table to him. Stepping into the vee of his legs, she dropped to her knees to wrap her arms around his middle and hug him to her. "I'm so sorry, James. I never meant to make you feel that way. You weren't alone. You . . ." She shook her head and tilted it up to him. "You rocked my world. Left me on a shaky axis. I *still* feel it even now. Do you?"

His eyes remained serious, but the corners of his mouth twitched slightly. "To tell you the truth, with you in that position . . . same."

She snorted and he pulled her up and into his lap, cuddling her into him. "I've always been the one to pursue you sexually," he said into her hair. "Then last night I was enough of a hypocrite to be annoyed when I thought you saw me as nothing else. I didn't like how that felt between us."

"It wasn't that. It was never that." She cupped his face. "I like your brain and your smile as much as I like your favorite body part."

That got a laugh out of him. "Same. I like your brain and your smile as much as I like *all* your body parts." He kissed her softly. "I get that you're here because you're worried about losing your dad. I know the feeling."

She knew he did. He'd lost a piece of himself when he'd lost Jason. She couldn't imagine the pain of that. "I don't know what I'd do if I lost him," she admitted.

"But see, he's right here in front of you. We all are." He cupped her face. "Can you say the same? Are you a hundred percent here with us?"

She looked into his eyes and saw only acceptance, affection, and concern for her. "I think we both know I need to work on that," she said softly.

"Actually, I need to work on several things. But the good news is, once I set my mind to something, I don't give up until I've got it right."

He smiled. "Sounds promising."

She flashed a mischievous grin. "Some things take practice, though. Lots of it."

"Good thing I'm really good at practicing . . ."

Chapter Eleven

JAMES DIDN'T often let himself think of the future. After all, he knew better than most that not everyone got one. But being with Hannah again, he couldn't help but think of the one he'd once upon a time hoped to have with her.

It was afternoon beneath a warm sun, nothing but the Caribbean Sea for miles, and his favorite girl in a different bikini, this one a heart-stopping red. They were currently sitting on the swim deck off the back of the boat, dripping wet and breathing hard from a race, winner to collect the spoils of their choice. Hannah had beaten him, mostly because he couldn't take his eyes off her as she swam, moving through the water while laughing so hard that she'd nearly drowned herself.

She was still laughing when she pushed her drenched hair from her face and met his gaze, her smile slowly fading.

"What?" he asked.

"I'm really sorry about this morning."

"I don't need an apology," he said. He knew her well. When she wanted something badly enough, she made it happen for herself. If he was ever lucky enough to have it be *him* she wanted again, she'd let him know. "It's okay, Hannah."

"No, it's not. I put work ahead of you and I shouldn't have. It didn't mean I didn't want to be with you, not then and not at breakfast."

"Work has been your life for a long time. It's understandable that you'd put it first."

"Well . . ." She smiled. "I'm not working right *now*."

That adorably sexy smile was something his body remembered quite well, and damn, he loved Playful Sexy Hannah. "You're not," he said with a laugh. "And you have yet to claim your prize— even though you cheated."

"I'd never cheat." But she laughed.

"Uh-huh," he said, unable to keep from laughing with her. She was . . . *infectious*. "So when you had a quick bikini-top malfunction out there and flashed me, that was entirely by accident?"

She lifted her chin, but her eyes revealed both heat and humor. "I don't know what you're talking about."

He moved closer, crowding her for the simple pleasure of having her close as he smiled into her face. "Maybe we should discuss this later in private, in greater detail."

"I agree," she said. "Lying down, in case I get . . . tired."

"I like the way you think." He touched the tip of her nose. "You need more sunblock." He sat up and reached for the bottle.

"You just want to get your hands on me again."

"One hundred percent. Lie down on your front."

She hurried to do just that, wriggling into place and making him groan because she had the cutest, sexiest wedgie going. All too aware of the fact that her dad might very well have eyes on them, he did his best to make this a PG event, keeping his hands on her sun-warmed skin and not slipping beneath the itty-bitty bikini.

"I've got to tell my dad in the morning before we hit San Juan," she murmured, eyes closed. "And then your parents will be here and you'll have a chance to talk to your dad as well. Big day."

"Yeah."

She slipped her hand in his and sighed. "Back to real life."

He drew a deep breath but didn't say anything, and she looked over at him.

"I remember the last time we were lying right here," he said.

She sat up and nodded. "It'd been a hard year for both of us."

"Yeah," he said. "My brother had died and the girl I loved dumped me and then ghosted me. As hard as a year ever gets."

She stared at him. "You . . . loved me?"

"Does it matter now?"

She drew a deep breath. "Yes. And I didn't dump you. It . . . didn't work out."

He snorted.

"It didn't!" She pointed at him. "You wanted me to walk away from a college internship and travel the world, no questions asked, no plans, just fly by the seat of your pants. And I got that you were coming from a place of overwhelming grief, I really did, but I wanted . . . no, I *needed* to go home and take that internship so I could set myself up for the future. I understood what you had to do, but you didn't even try to understand what I needed to do. You wanted to be happy. But everyone experiences happiness in different ways, James. Hard work and stability are more important to me than happiness. So is having a safety net."

"It wasn't just what I wanted, Hannah." He paused and drew a deep breath because the last thing he wanted was for this week to end like the last one they were together. "I promised Jason that I'd spend New Year's in Barbados, a place he'd always wanted to go, but could never get away from work to do it."

She stared at him. "What?"

"Yeah, because at the end, he realized some things. That he'd worked too hard and too long and had never lived his life."

She looked stunned. "You never said . . ."

"It'd been his choice, of course. But in the end, he knew he'd made mistakes. He had regrets, because he'd never done any of the things he would've put on a bucket list, including falling in love and having kids. He was always working and looking ahead, never in the moment." He swallowed hard. "He made me promise I wouldn't do that, that I'd live doing something that made me happy."

"I . . . didn't know that."

"I know," he said. "I told myself you never gave me the chance to tell you about it, but honestly?" He shrugged. "I guess I really just wanted you to choose me because you wanted to be with me, not because I guilted you into it with a promise I'd made to Jason."

A tear slid down her cheek. "I wasn't capable of making that decision," she whispered. "Or even of traveling with you, because I knew the truth—that if I talked to you about it, I'd have walked away from the internship, no looking back. And I couldn't live a Peter Pan life, James. I had to grow up."

And there it was. He nodded. "Because one of us had to, right?"

She grimaced. "I didn't mean it like that."

"You did, but that's okay." He rose to his feet. "We each did what we had to do. No regrets, right?"

Some emotion crossed her face, but she cleared her expression and gave him a tight nod.

From a lower deck, Sally called out for James.

"Coming," he called back, eyes on Hannah. Waiting for her to say . . . shit, he had no idea. But she said nothing, and he nodded, then walked away.

Chapter Twelve

Watching James walk away, Hannah felt her heart break in two all over again. *He'd loved her . . .*

"Smalls."

She kept her back to her dad. "It's not a good time," she managed to say.

"I just got a message from your mom."

She closed her eyes, concentrating on the warm breeze caressing her face and the squawk of happy birds.

"WTF didn't you tell me?" Harry asked.

She let out a mirthless laugh and dropped her head back to look up at the perfectly gorgeous blue sky. Where was a moody storm when she needed one? "Still not using that right, Dad."

"Your mom's divorcing me?"

Oh shit. She turned to face him and wanted to cry all over again at the look of utter devastation on his face.

"So it's true?"

"I meant to tell you," she whispered.

"So why didn't you?"

"I . . ." There was no excuse. None. "I was trying to find the right time."

He gaped at her, hurt and disbelief in every line of his body. "The right time would've been the minute you boarded this boat. But you were too busy with that contraption that's always glued to your ear."

Yeah, and *that contraption* was going off as she stood there. The hearing was coming up in a few hours, but she kept her hand out of her pocket and her eyes on her dad. "You know that the only reason I got the time off from work to be here with you for Christmas was by promising my boss I'd work remotely to have her back on this case."

"I didn't want you on this boat for Christmas." He pointed at her. "I wanted *you* for Christmas. I wanted to spend time like we used to, doing the things we both love. I've missed you, and I rarely get to see you." He shook his head. "I don't know why I'm surprised. Your mom was always too busy for me too, and I guess the apple never falls far from the tree, right?"

She'd been worried about falling once again for the sexy wanderlusting James, worried about her dad's impending divorce pain, worried about keeping up with work . . . worried about everything but her own actions. As a result, her dad was right. She *had* been acting a lot like her mom, putting everything before the important stuff, such as caring for the people in her life.

Not that this epiphany did anything for the

hurt now coursing through her at her dad's harsh words. "I learned from *both* of my parents," she told him. "Yes, Mom was so busy with her life that we rarely got time with her, but you were busy too, Dad, with the boat. I'm not sure exactly what *you're* remembering, but *I'm* recalling your telling me to go be good and keep myself busy while you worked. From a young age, I had to keep myself occupied and out of your way. So really, there were *two* trees I didn't fall far from." With her phone still going off, she stood. "I'm sorry for all of it. I should have told you, but I wasn't in all that much of a hurry to hurt you." She pulled out her phone and looked at her screen. "Now I've got to get this." Turning away, she answered Cynthia's call.

"Hannah, thank god. The hearing's on hold because there's a problem. We're missing two signed affidavits from the surgeon. There won't be a ruling or a surgery unless we get those."

Hannah frowned. "Right, but I talked about this with your assistant yesterday morning, who assured me she'd go get them."

"I didn't think we'd need them. I heard otherwise last night, and my assistant texted you, letting you know I needed you to handle this. You're the only one who can get through to the surgeon that fast. So . . . where are we with that?"

Seemed like her entire world was going to crash in on itself today. "I didn't get a text from her or I'd have reminded you both that someone needed to go in person. Ideally it'd be someone familiar enough with the surgeon and staff to expedite the process."

"Yes, and that would be you."

"Which would require my getting on a plane."

"Perfect," Cynthia said. "I'll tell everyone you're on it."

Hannah let out a low, mirthless laugh. "You want me to fly back? I'm on a boat."

"Your itinerary says you'll be in Puerto Rico in a few hours. I'm going to have to get the hearing pushed until tomorrow. Plenty of time for you to get a red-eye back here."

"But . . . Hello?" She stared at her phone. Perfect. Cynthia had hung up. Hannah looked up at her dad. "I suppose you caught the gist of that."

He turned on his heel and walked away.

Awesome. Two for two today.

Five minutes later Cynthia's assistant called her to facilitate flights and ground transportation. When she ended the call, she turned and found her dad once again standing there, hands in his pockets, face unusually solemn.

"I shouldn't have walked away like that," he said, surprising her. "I'm sorry. Do you have time to talk before you go?"

She nodded, and he led her across the deck to the sun chairs. They both sat and he looked at her. "I want you to know I heard what you said to me, and I'm sorry for a lot of things. Can I tell you about them?"

"Always."

He nodded, looking grateful. "Sometimes it seems like the harder I try to get things right, the more I screw everything up."

"Dad," she said wearily, "you didn't screw anything up."

"Hold on, Smalls. Let me finish. A few days ago I told you that nothing's free, but that wasn't true. My love for you is free."

Her throat tightened and her eyes stung. "Same," she whispered.

His eyes looked shiny now as well, and he cleared his throat. "What I *should've* said to you is that I'm sorry your mom and I put you in a position where you had to be the one to deliver the news. And even more sorry that I always chose my boat over you."

"You didn't always."

He smiled sadly and tugged on a loose strand of her hair. "You're the sweetest thing in my life, do you know that?" He sighed. "The truth is that life's about hard choices, about choosing what's right over what's fun, and we both know that's never been my strong suit." He put his elbows to his knees and leaned in, his eyes more serious than she'd ever seen them. "I got mad at you for putting your work ahead of me, when I'd done the exact same thing to you for years. Not putting you ahead of my boat is one of the two biggest regrets of my life. The other one is not picking you and your mom when she gave her ultimatum—her or the boat. I won't ever do that to you again. I promise you."

Sniffing back tears, she reached for his hand. "I told myself I was coming here for you, to be there for you when I had to tell you the news. But the truth is, I also came here for me. Once you sign those papers, I'm not your stepdaughter anymore, and I wasn't ready for that to be true."

With a rough sound of grief, he tugged her out of her chair and in for a hard hug. "A piece of paper isn't what makes us family," he whispered against her hair.

Unable to speak, she just nodded, wrapping her arms tight around him.

"You're stuck with me, Hannah. More than just for Christmas."

"More than just for Christmas," she whispered, fiercely grateful for that, for him.

Pulling back, he quickly swiped a forearm over his wet eyes, then met her gaze. "There're so many things I've neglected in bringing you up. I never even taught you how to ride a bike."

"No, but thanks to you, I know how to make every different kind of knot under the sun, how to jury-rig anything with MacGyver-level skill, and how to handle a seventy-foot-long ship. How many people can say that?"

"But how practical is that? When you learned to drive a car, I should've made sure you knew how to change a tire."

"I've got Triple A for that. But there's no Triple A for mooring in a busy harbor without hitting anything. I can pull into a slip in a windstorm without so much as a scratch," she said proudly. "I can do that and more."

"True." He rubbed the scruff on his jaw, a tell that revealed when he was about to say something uncomfortable for him. "I also never threatened any of your boyfriends about behaving themselves. Or . . ."

She stared at him. "Are you blushing?"

"Jesus." He swiped a hand across his face. "Yes, apparently. I'm trying to say that we never had . . . the talk. You know, about being safe. And protected."

Hannah gaped at him. "No need to have the birds-and-bees talk at this point. Dad, that ship sailed a long time ago."

He smiled sheepishly and nearly sagged with relief. "Thank god, because to be honest, I think I've forgotten more than I remember."

She laughed. "You almost just scarred the both of us for life."

With a chuckle, he shook his head. "Yeah, thanks for stopping me." His smile faded and his gaze searched hers. "So . . . we're okay?"

She hugged him again. "We're okay."

"Good." He nodded. "So now you can go do whatever it is that you need to."

"With work or with James?"

"Well, I'd be lying if I didn't say I hope you work

things out with James, but I'm not going to inter-
fere."

She drew a deep breath. "I don't think we *can*
work things out."

He scowled. "What are you talking about? It's
obvious to anyone with eyes in their head that
you two love each other. You've *always* loved each
other."

She smiled sadly. "Yes, but we both know that
love isn't always enough."

He let out a ragged breath. "Yeah."

"I'm sorry Mom hurt you," she said quietly.

"No, I can't let you put it all on her. I hurt her
plenty too, and frankly, I waited way too long to
fix my wrongs. I got what I deserved." He shook
his shaggy head. "I screwed up my happy ending,
but you don't have to do the same." He gave her
a tight smile. "I'd tell you to learn from your old
man, but the truth is, we all have to make our own
mistakes."

"Well, don't you worry, I've made plenty," she
quipped. *"Recently* . . . Dad . . . I'm worried about
leaving you here alone on Christmas . . ."

"I'm not alone. Sally's here. James too, and soon
his parents. I said I wanted you to do what you
need to, and I meant it."

She kissed his cheek. "Thanks, Dad."

"We'll hit land within two hours, so you should
probably go pack."

Hannah nodded and started to walk away, but
then she turned back. "Dad?

"Yeah, Smalls?"

She smiled. "Whenever you do get back on that bike, if you need the talk, I'll be there for you."

He was laughing when she walked away this time. She was smiling too, even though her heart hurt like hell.

Chapter Thirteen

JAMES STOOD at the top of the passerelle beside the moored *Therapist*. They were in the port of San Juan in Puerto Rico, and he was watching out for his parents when he finally saw them coming down the main dock toward him.

His heart, trampled on and hurting, still managed to clutch at seeing the joy on their faces at the sight of him. His mom got him in a tight hug, squeezing the air from his lungs, holding on when he tried to pull away. Finally, with a small laugh, he gave in, letting her hug him half to death.

"He's turning purple," his dad said.

His mom pulled back and kissed James on both cheeks, then narrowed her eyes and frowned. "What's wrong?" She noticed the duffel bag at his feet and her frown deepened.

James hugged his dad and then looked at both his parents. "I'm sorry, but I'm not staying."

"Susan, talk to your son."

His mom didn't take her eyes off James. "How about we let him talk instead?"

"There's no talking on vacation," his dad said.

James's mom turned to look at her husband. "Honey, you have avoided this as long as possible. It's not fair."

His dad sighed heavily. "Yeah." He turned to James. "Okay, let's sit."

They boarded and sat on the deck beneath a warm sun, surrounded by the bustle of the harbor around them. His parents looked at him, his mom worried, his dad . . . resigned.

"I know this is going to sound sudden," James said. "But please know I've given this a lot of thought. Dad . . ."—he drew a deep breath—"I don't want to take over Webber Lumber. I know you had high hopes for Jason. Instead you've had to make do with me, and I've never been as dedicated as he was or nearly as good. But the fact is, I can't be like him because I'm *not* him."

His dad, looking devastated, made a sound of regret.

"Told you," Susan said with a soft reproach before reaching for James's hand. "Baby, listen to me very carefully. We don't want you to be Jason. We've *never* wanted that."

"We've never wanted you to be anything but you," his dad said, voice thick with emotion.

"You mean that?"

"*More than anything.*" His dad rubbed a hand to his chest. "I thought you were going to tell me you were going off to do your own thing and weren't going to have any more time for us."

Some of what felt like two tons of weight came

off James's own chest. "Of course not. I'd never walk away from you, from either of you."

His mom wiped a few tears and hugged him tight.

His dad did the same. "You're not the only one who came to some hard realizations after we lost Jason. Mine's simple—life's too damn short to be anything other than happy." He paused. "But you sure don't look happy right now. And I know that look. It's about a woman, isn't it."

"Dan," his mom said quietly.

"Well, it is." He turned back to James. "Right?"

James blew out a sigh. "Tell me I'm not that easy to read."

"It's Hannah," his mom guessed.

"Okay," James muttered, "so I *am* that easy to read."

"You two admit you're in love yet?" his mom asked hopefully, and James knew that Hannah had been right to try and hide their . . . well, whatever the hell it'd been between them, or their moms would absolutely have already had their wedding planned.

"It's not what you think," he said. "She . . . well, she left me." He paused because actually, technically *he'd* been the one to actually leave, but she'd been the one to *mentally* go first.

"Son, when it comes to love, everyone walks away a time or two. Sometimes you're the one to go, and other times you'll be the one doing the chasing."

"And the groveling," his mom added with a meaningful look at his dad.

"Obviously I've done my share of both," his dad said wryly. "That's how relationships work. The system falls apart only when you're both too stubborn to go after the other person. And I *know* you're not too stubborn for love because you're a Webber."

"Aw," his mom murmured, "that's so sweet."

James stared at his dad.

His dad gave a half-smile. "I can't actually tell if you're stunned by my brilliance or your own stupidity."

"I think it might be a little of both," James admitted. "When did you get so wise?"

"It's called old age, and don't go there, it's a trick. James, do you love her?"

That was easy. "Yes."

"Then what are you doing sitting here? Go after her."

"I've done that."

"Yeah? How did it go?"

James opened his mouth, but then shut it again and sat back, realizing he'd *never* gone after Hannah. Not once. He'd always expected her to be there on his terms, never returning the favor. He'd expected her to give up everything and go away with him, then blamed her for their demise when she wouldn't do it. That was on him, for not bringing her all the way in on why he needed to go, what he'd promised Jason. Instead, he'd assumed she'd follow him on blind faith, without understanding what it meant to him.

What a hypocritical dick.

But he was tired of running. Jason was gone and nobody could bring him back, so maybe it was time to actually live by the motto his brother had pushed. He needed to get his own happy—which happened to be one imperfectly perfect brunette with warm brown eyes and a sweet smile. He stood up and looked down at his parents.

His mom waved him off. "Don't worry about us. I'm defrosting for the first time in a month. We'll be fine."

"Go," his dad said.

So he went. He ran the length of the passerelle to the dock while pulling out his phone to get a ride to the airport, only to stop short ten feet from the ship because Hannah was running toward him, looking like she was both laughing and crying. He pulled her into him. "What's wrong? Are you okay?"

"Yes. *No*," she corrected, shaking her head, gasping for air. "I need to hit the gym more."

As stunned as he was, he couldn't find the humor in that statement to save his life. "Hannah, what are you doing?"

"I was leaving, but I made the cab turn around," she said. "I needed to see you."

He shook his head, dizzy with relief to see her, but afraid to hope. "But the case—your dad told me about the affidavits you need—"

"I've developed working relationships with most of the medical staff at my hospital. I called the surgeon's office and begged to talk to him. His office is doing the paperwork as I speak, and Cynthia will personally go get them. It should be okay."

He was boggled. "Why aren't you going?"

She took a deep breath. "Because I forgot to tell you something."

Okay, this could be really bad or really good, and since luck hadn't been on his side lately, he braced himself. "That's funny," he said as lightly as he could. "I need to tell you something too."

"Can I go first?" she asked very seriously. "Because I'm going to disintegrate into a million pieces unless I say this to you." She let her purse and duffel hit the deck and cupped his face. "You're more important to me than a job, and I'm sorry I didn't show you that. I was . . ."—she shook her head—"scared. I've buried myself in work for so long . . . I've forgotten how to leave space for the people I care about."

He opened his mouth, but she put a finger to his lips. "Because of that, I've never let a guy all the way in. I mean, how could I when it involved stuff like . . . being home for dinner and pretending not to care if the other person refuses to put the toilet seat down." She swallowed. "And then there's the biggest problem of all."

"What's that?"

"I've used up every single inch of my closet. *And* all of the shelves in the whole apartment."

The hope he'd been attempting to keep reined in broke free and a rough laugh escaped him. His knees nearly buckled in relief as he spoke around Hannah's fingers still against his mouth. "Okay, but those aren't actual problems. We will find time to have meals together, and I live out of a duffel bag for long stretches of time, so I'll never care about closet space. Also, I can go either way on the toilet seat. What I can't go either way on is *you*."

She exhaled and sagged into him. "You just did in my knees."

"I've got you. I know I've screwed that up before, but I've got you now, Hannah. I'm at your back, always."

She had her hands fisted in his shirt, staring up at him. "There's still an actual real problem."

Not if he could help it, he thought, stroking a strand of hair from her face. "Lay it on me, Hannah Banana."

"I've never been able to make a relationship work. Never, not once, James," she said, clearly a hundred percent serious. "And there's something else. I'm . . . *difficult*." She whispered the word, as if she was ashamed of that.

A wave of affection and a fierce sense of protectiveness for this prickly woman he loved more than life itself overcame him. Covering her hands with his, he smiled at her. "And . . . ?"

"And"—she bit her lower lip, looking nervous and anxious—"and people don't tend to like that."

His amusement was gone in a blink, replaced by

so much emotion his chest didn't feel like it could contain it all. "Hannah, I love that about you."

She stared at him like he'd grown a second head. "You love that I'm difficult?"

"I love the fact that you have your own mind and speak it. I love how passionate you are and how you dig in your heels on the things that matter most to you."

"But . . . what if you stop?" she asked with heartbreaking emotion in her voice. "What if you stop loving those things about me?"

Pulling her into him, he dropped his forehead to hers. He looked into her eyes, and the emotion and love he read there filled his soul and dismissed all the doubts he'd ever had about being enough for her. "Babe, I've loved you for all these years. That's not going to change now. Or ever." He paused. "I've got some more things to say now. Will you listen?"

She stared into his eyes. "Yes."

Do not blow this. "When I saw you running toward me on the dock just now, I felt the greatest relief in my life. I want you to know that even if you hadn't come back, I was coming to you. I was wrong to walk away from you. And I was wrong six years ago too, asking you to drop your life for mine. That wasn't fair, and it wasn't something a man should do to the woman he loves."

She opened her mouth, but he gently set *his* finger to *her* lips. "And I do love you, Hannah. I love you and I should've fought for you, for both of us,

after Jason died and on this trip as well. I'm sorry
I didn't, but I can promise you, I'll never not fight
for you again."

"*Same*," she said finally, the sweetest promise
he'd ever heard. "But, James, I still live in Wildstone. You live . . . well, sometimes you're in New
York helping your dad, but mostly you're gone,
working all over the world."

"That's all true, but for a while now, I've known
I needed a home base. I'm yearning for that, actually."

She blinked. "You are?"

"Yes. And I'm thinking the smartest home base
would be Wildstone. See, there's a woman there I
love and need in my life."

She was staring up at him. "But what about your
job?"

"There's an airport for when I need to run an
expedition, but I'm going to be doubling my staff.
I won't be gone nearly as much."

"But . . . that'd be changing your whole life. I
don't want you to do that, not for me."

"I'd do anything for you." He cupped her face. "I
love you, Hannah."

Her hands came up to cover his, her voice soft
but firm. "I love you too, James. I always have. And
I don't know why I'm only just now saying that to
you. I've felt it forever."

He smiled, feeling the last of the pieces of his
damaged heart slide into place. "Maybe it's finally
the right time."

She stepped into him, slid her arms around his neck and pulled him down for a kiss.

"You're my home base, Hannah. For now and forever, if you'll have me."

She smiled. "Remember yesterday when I won, but never claimed my spoils?"

Puzzled, he nodded. "Yeah."

"You're it. I claim you, James. You're it for me, for now and forever."

Epilogue

One year later

Iт was the night before Christmas and all through the boat, not a creature was stirring . . . Hannah stood on deck, Harry at her side. Together they were taking in the view, which was different this year.

Very different.

They weren't surrounded by the Caribbean, but were on the Pacific coast. Which meant that instead of blue-green seas for as far as the eye could see, they were in Morro Bay, surrounded by the gorgeous California green rolling hills.

The boat was, of course, *The Therapist*. Hannah smiled at Harry and then took in everyone else as well, seated along both sides of the walkway so that it was now a makeshift aisle. Her mom and her new husband. Sally, who was wearing an engagement ring from none other than Harry himself. Susan and Dan.

And James, standing at the other end, under a

wooden arch that he'd built for her, waiting for her to walk down the aisle to him. He was watching her, a small just-for-her smile on his lips, his eyes filled with so much love she had to swallow hard as emotion nearly overwhelmed her.

The year had gone by so fast. Her boss had been promoted, and so had she, taking Cynthia's old job, giving her more of an administrative position. Which in turn freed her up to work from home—or better yet, to travel when she wanted to tag along with James. She'd been able to untether herself from the job a bit, while still making sure the cases that needed to be heard were heard.

As for her almost husband, one of the first things he'd done was convince Harry to come work for him. Harry had happily shifted his life to be closer to Hannah's.

But the biggest thing James had done was stand by his word. He'd opened a home office in Wildstone, and because Wildstone was virtually a playground in itself, he'd created a series of adventures right in Hannah's backyard, working for a variety of clients big and small who wanted to provide their employees with exclusive and unique team-building experiences.

He and Hannah had bought a small house, and she'd thought nothing could make her happier than all of last year. Except now, standing there about to walk to the man of her dreams and exchange vows, she knew that she'd been wrong. This, the official entangling of their lives, filled her heart in a way she could never have imagined.

"Ready, Smalls?" Harry asked.

She'd never been more ready for anything in her life.

rainy day friends
978-0-06-296319-2

Six months after Lanie Jacobs' husband's death, she takes a job at
a family-run winery. They all take her under their wing, especially
Mark Capriotti, a gruffly handsome deputy sheriff who winds his
way into Lanie's cold, broken heart.

wrapped up in you
978-0-06-289778-7

Ivy Snow's reinvented life is on solid ground, and she's
guarded against anything that can rock it. Like Idaho sheriff
Kel O'Donnell. Too hot not to set off alarms, he screams
temporary. If only his whispers weren't so delightfully
naughty and irresistible.

lost and found sisters
978-0-06-293791-9

Quinn Weller gives up job, home, and boyfriend and heads to
Wildstone, California. Though she doesn't fit in at first, she's
drawn to the small town . . . and the handsome, dark-haired
stranger who offers friendship with no questions asked.

playing for keeps
978-0-06-274188-2

When it comes to Caleb Parker, Sadie Lane feels the spark—the
kind that comes from rubbing each other the wrong way. But after they accidentally co-rescue an abandoned dog from a storm,
Sadie sees a vulnerable side to the seemingly invincible hottie.

JS2 0621